Invasion of the Body Squeezers

Part I

Look for more books in the Goosebumps Series 2000
by R.L. Stine:

#1 Cry of the Cat
#2 Bride of the Living Dummy
#3 Creature Teacher

Invasion of the Body Squeezers

Part I

AN
APPLE
PAPERBACK

SCHOLASTIC INC.
New York Toronto London Auckland Sydney

A PARACHUTE PRESS BOOK

ISBN 0-590-39991-8

Copyright © 1998 by Parachute Press, Inc.
All rights reserved. Published by Scholastic Inc.
APPLE PAPERBACKS and logo are trademarks and/or registered trademarks of Scholastic Inc.
GOOSEBUMPS is a registered trademark
of Parachute Press, Inc.

12 11 10 9 8 7 6 5 4 3 2 1   8 9/9 0 1 2 3/0

Printed in the U.S.A.

First Scholastic printing, April 1998

ometimes I think my sister is an alien from another planet.

Her name is Billie, and she is seven. She looks like a normal kid — small, kind of skinny, curly blonde hair, and big brown eyes — like me.

But it's hard to imagine that a normal kid from Earth could be such a huge *pain*!

The problem is Billie has to compete. Even though I'm twelve, she has to be better than me in everything! No matter what, she has to be the first, the best, the fastest!

Does it drive me crazy?

Take a guess.

Take today. We were sitting in the den, staring at the TV. Sharing a bowl of potato chips.

"Hey, look, Billie," I said, holding up a potato

chip as big as my hand. "Check out the size of this chip."

"Big deal, Jack. I had one *twice* as big," Billie replied.

I sighed. "I've already seen this show," I told her.

"I've already seen it *three* times!" she exclaimed.

"I'm getting a stomachache from all these chips," I groaned.

She groaned too. "I'm getting a stomachache *and* a headache."

Get the picture?

Normal Earthlings don't think like that — *do* they?

I took another handful of chips and stared at the screen. We were watching a wildlife show called *Fangs*, because Billie likes to watch animals eat other animals. Actually, I like to watch that too. But mostly I'm into space, the unknown. . . .

I shoved the greasy chips into my mouth and watched a mountain lion chew on a deer. Suddenly, the animals vanished. A sign came up on the screen: SPECIAL NEWS BULLETIN.

"Bring back the mountain lion!" Billie protested. "We just got to the good part!"

"Sshhhh." I pressed my hand over her mouth. I like to hear special news bulletins.

A serious-looking woman appeared on the screen. "We have a special bulletin from NASA

2

headquarters," she said. "An unknown object has entered Earth's orbit."

"Billie, it's your spaceship. They're coming for you!" I teased.

"They're coming for *you*, Saucerman!" she shot back.

"Don't call me that!" I snapped angrily.

Why did Billie call me Saucerman? *No way* I'm telling.

I turned back to the TV. "According to NASA, the object could be a comet or a meteor," the woman reported. "It is very large. NASA scientists are surprised that it did not burn up when it entered our atmosphere."

They cut to a man in a white lab coat. He pulled off his eyeglasses and rubbed his eyes. "If it *is* a comet," he said, "it's one we've never seen before."

"Cool!" I cried, jumping up from the couch. "I would *love* to see a real comet!"

"I've already seen a comet," Billie sneered. "No. I've seen *two* comets!"

Do you *believe* her?

Do you see why sometimes there are *major fights* in the Archer family?

I tossed a couch pillow at her. "Stop bragging all the time," I said. "And stop making up stories."

Her brown eyes flashed. She grinned. "Okay, Saucerman," she replied.

"Aaaaagh!" I let out an exasperated groan and started out of the den. Behind me on the TV, the mountain lion was back, gobbling away on the deer.

"Jack — where are you going?" Billie demanded.

"I'm going to spy on Mr. Fleshman," I replied.

"Again?"

I nodded. "Something very weird is going on over there," I told her.

Mr. Fleshman moved into the house next door a few months ago. He is tall and really scary-looking. He has very tanned skin. He has silvery hair cut very short and silver-gray eyes. They're so light, you can barely see his pupils.

He wears black all the time. Black sport shirts and black pants. He drives a little black convertible. Not that he drives it much. He stays home most of the time.

Mr. Fleshman isn't very friendly. He never says hi when he sees me in the backyard. I don't think he's talked to Mom or Dad much, either. He keeps to himself in that big, old house.

One night a few weeks ago, I was up in my room. I was leaning out my bedroom window, checking out the sky with binoculars. I like to search for shooting stars and satellites and things.

When I looked down, I could see clearly into one of Mr. Fleshman's back windows. And I nearly dropped my binoculars when I saw . . . *some kind of creature.*

4

I only got a glimpse of it before it moved away from the window. But I know what I saw.

It stood on two legs, big as a bear. I couldn't tell if it was human or animal. It had wet, grayish flesh that hung loosely, as if rotting off its bones. One side of its face appeared smashed in. One eye dangled in front of it.

And it was *alive*.

I think.

I'm not sure about any of this. As I said, I only had a two-second glimpse.

I've been spying on Mr. Fleshman's house ever since.

"Did you see the creature again?" Billie asked from the couch.

"I only saw it that one time," I told her. "But maybe today —"

"I saw it too," Billie interrupted. "Actually, I saw *four* creatures!"

I didn't say anything. I made a face at her. Then I hurried up to my room for the binoculars.

A wooden picket fence runs between our two yards. It used to be white, but Dad hasn't painted it in a long while. So it's faded and peeling. Some of the boards are missing.

I like to squeeze into a hole where two boards are gone, duck down, and spy on Mr. Fleshman's back windows.

I squinted into the hazy afternoon sunlight. The lemon trees behind Mom's flower garden had ripe lemons on the branches. Some of the flowers appeared dry and wilted.

On TV, they said this was one of the hottest summers on record in Los Angeles. As I crossed the lawn, the hot sun made the back of my neck prickle. I wiped the sweat off my forehead.

Mom and Dad rented a house on the beach in Malibu. But they've been working so hard this summer, we've only been to it once.

I stepped up to the hole in the fence and checked out the kitchen window. Did something move behind the white curtain?

Was it the creature?

I started to raise the binoculars — when something else caught my eye.

Something moving across the sky.

"Huh?" I let out a gasp. The binoculars fell from my hand.

A round object up there. Glowing like gold.

The comet?

Oh, no!

It was swooping down so fast!

No time to run. No time to duck.

I raised both hands to shield myself — and opened my mouth in a horrified scream as it bounced off my head!

2

"OWWWWW!"

It hit the fence. And bounced across Mr. Fleshman's backyard.

Dizzy, I staggered hard against the fence. Struggled to catch my balance.

I rubbed my head — and watched the ball roll to a stop in front of Mr. Fleshman's back porch.

The ball?

Yes. Not a comet. Not a blazing meteorite from outer space. A gold, rubber ball. About the size of a soccer ball.

Still leaning against the fence, I shut my eyes and waited for the laughter. I knew it would come. And sure enough, I heard it.

I opened my eyes to find four kids from my class laughing and hooting. Enjoying their little joke.

Maddy Wiener lives across the street. Marsha

James lives two houses down from her. Derek Lee and Henry Glover live in Westwood, but they go to our school.

"Give me a break!" I grumbled. "You guys aren't funny."

"Sure we are!" Derek declared. He slapped Henry a two-handed high five.

"What are you doing back here?" Maddy demanded. Maddy is pretty awesome-looking. She has long, frizzed-out black hair, blue eyes, and pouty lips. She's acted in some commercials and does some modeling.

Her best friend, Marsha, has curly red hair and a face full of freckles. She's very quiet. Maddy talks enough for both of them!

I raised a finger to my lips. "Sshhh." I peered cautiously over the fence. "There's something weird going on in that house."

Henry laughed. "There's something weird going on in *your* house, Jack. It's *you*!"

The four of them thought that was a riot. They hooted and laughed some more.

"I'm serious!" I cried. "I saw some kind of creature in there."

"You mean like a dog?" Maddy asked.

"No. I mean like a *creature*," I replied. "It had rotting, gray skin and a crushed-in skull, and a long, animal-like snout, and —"

Henry turned to Marsha. "He was looking in *your* window, Marsha!"

8

The others laughed. Marsha gave Henry a hard shove into the fence. "*You're* the only one with a long snout, Glover!"

That shut Henry up. He's very sensitive about his big, crooked nose.

Henry and Derek are both big guys — big heads, big chests, tall and athletic-looking. They're both on the soccer and the swim teams at school.

Henry is a little funny-looking with his tiny, black eyes and crooked beak. And he wears bright blue braces on his teeth.

Derek has a round, almost pudgy face, short black hair, and dark, mischievous eyes. Derek always appears to be thinking of something funny.

I kind of like all four of these kids. But they really give me a hard time.

"Why don't you believe me about the creature?" I demanded, glancing at Mr. Fleshman's window.

Was something peering back at me? I ducked down behind the fence.

"Why don't we believe you?" Derek demanded. "Why don't we believe you?"

"Because you're you!" Maddy declared.

"Give me another reason," I replied.

"You're always talking about weird things," Marsha said.

"Like what?" I demanded.

"Okay. Mr. Potter," Derek said.

"Excuse me?" I cried. "Mr. Potter? You mean that substitute teacher?"

Derek nodded. "Remember? You said he was a werewolf? You told everyone in school he was a werewolf? And it turned out he was just trying to grow a beard?"

They all laughed.

"Okay, okay. I messed up on that one," I confessed.

"And the flying saucer?" Marsha chimed in. "Don't forget the flying saucer."

"Whoa — !" I raised a hand to stop them. But I knew they wouldn't stop.

"You showed everyone that Polaroid snapshot of a flying saucer," Maddy said, shaking her head. "And it was a street lamp half-hidden by a tree."

Henry slapped me on the back. "Way to go, Saucerman!"

They laughed again. I laughed too. It *was* pretty funny.

Okay. Okay. So now you know why they call me Saucerman.

"This time I know I'm right," I insisted. "This time I saw it with my own eyes. There's something very weird going on in that house. I saw an ugly creature in that back window. I really did."

I picked up the binoculars. I glanced in Mr. Fleshman's back window.

And saw two eyes staring out at me!

"There it is!" I cried, turning back to them.

10

"Quick. Check out the window! Do you see it? *Do* you?"

My four friends peered over the fence.

I watched their expressions change.

I watched their eyes bulge in shock. And I watched their mouths open in startled cries.

"Oh, wow!" Maddy gasped. "Oh, wow!"

I spun around — and saw what they were gaping at.

Mr. Fleshman stood on his back porch, dressed in black, hands on his waist. He stared angrily across the yard at us with his strange, silvery eyes.

He didn't say a word. Without taking his eyes off us, he bent and picked up the gold rubber ball. Then he stood up, scowling at us, slapping the ball between his hands.

"I'm *outta* here!" Henry declared.

"No. Wait —" I started.

But all four of them took off. They scrambled across the street and didn't stop running until they disappeared behind Maddy's house.

I swallowed hard and turned back to Mr. Fleshman.

He was still scowling at me, his silvery eyes narrowed, moving the ball from one hand to the other.

Slap . . . slap . . . slap.

At dinner, I told Mom and Dad about Mr. Fleshman and the rubber ball. "He flashed me an evil stare," I said. I tried to imitate it.

Mom and Dad laughed. Billie imitated the stare too.

That made them laugh even harder.

"It isn't funny," I grumbled. "It was . . . scary."

"Mr. Fleshman seems to be a very private man," Mom commented. "I guess he doesn't like to have rubber balls bouncing over his lawn."

"What were you doing back there, anyway?" Dad asked.

"Well . . ." I hesitated. Should I tell them the truth? They were always scolding me for frightening Billie with my wild stories.

But I couldn't hold this one in.

"I was spying on his house," I blurted. "The other night, I saw some kind of . . . monster or something in there."

Mom held up a hand. "Jack — stop."

"No — really!" I cried. "I didn't get a real good look at it. But I saw it. It was —"

"I saw it too!" Billie chimed in. "A monster! No. I saw *two* monsters in there!"

"You did not!" I screamed. "You're so stupid!"

"Don't call your sister stupid," Mom warned.

Dad turned to Billie. "Stop trying to compete with your brother all the time. His stories are crazy enough without you making them even crazier."

"But — but — but —" I sputtered.

"You give your sister crazy ideas," Mom scolded. "She thinks she has to imitate you."

"That's because she's stupid," I grumbled.

No one ever believes me — all because of Billie.

"Pass the salad," Dad said.

"But I saw some kind of creature —" I protested.

"Fine. Pass the salad," Dad repeated.

That's what he does when he decides we're through talking about something. He says, "Pass the salad." That means *shut up*.

I grumbled to myself and passed him the salad bowl. My parents are on some kind of health kick, and we've been eating a *lot* of salad!

"What does Mr. Fleshman do, anyway?" Mom asked Dad.

Dad spooned a big heap of lettuce onto his plate. "I don't know," he replied. "He's not very friendly. I only talked with him once. He seemed a little strange. He —"

"A *little* strange?" I interrupted. "He's a total weirdo!"

Billie laughed. She had spaghetti sauce all over her chin.

Dad ignored me. "I think maybe Mr. Fleshman is just shy," he continued. "He seemed okay to me."

Mom squeezed my arm. "Stop spying on him, Jack. It really isn't nice to spy on a neighbor. Okay? Promise?"

I crossed my fingers under the table. "No problem," I said.

No way would I stop spying. Not until I found out the truth about the creature I saw and the truth about Mr. Fleshman.

After dinner, Mom and Dad went to a movie. Billie was over at a friend's house.

I was supposed to be reading one of my Summer Reading books for school. But I couldn't stop thinking about Mr. Fleshman and the creature.

I've got to take a peek inside that house, I decided.

But how?

An idea flashed instantly into my mind. Go over there and ask Mr. Fleshman for the ball back.

Excellent.

I hurried downstairs, taking the steps two at a time. Then I trotted across the backyard. I squeezed through the hole in the fence and made my way onto Mr. Fleshman's back porch.

The kitchen lights were on. And I could see lights in the other back windows.

He must be home, I decided.

I took a deep breath, cleared my throat — and knocked on the back door.

I waited a few seconds, listening for Mr. Fleshman's footsteps.

Maybe he's in the front and didn't hear me, I decided. I searched for a doorbell.

No. No bell.

So I raised my fist to pound on the door again.

My hand stopped in midair when I heard a low howl from inside the house.

What was that sound? A dog?

No. Mr. Fleshman doesn't own a dog.

Another howl made me jump back so fast, I nearly fell off the stoop.

The top half of the door was a window. I pressed my face against the glass and peered inside.

No one in the kitchen. On the far wall, I could see a doorway leading to a hall. I squinted my eyes, focusing on the doorway.

I heard a *THUD*. Then a groan.

Mr. Fleshman! He stumbled back into the wall. His arms flew up. His mouth was open in a choked scream.

What is going on? I wondered. Is he *fighting* with someone?

My heart pounded as I stared through the window.

I heard another heavy *THUD*.

A huge figure staggered into the hallway — and grabbed Mr. Fleshman by the throat.

The creature!

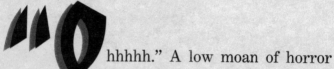

4

"**O**hhhh." A low moan of horror escaped my throat.

The creature — its decayed, gray flesh was dripping off its body. Its single eyeball bounced in front of its long snout.

Was it an animal? Was it human?

It moved like a human. But its head was crushed in. Crushed in. Crushed in . . .

My stomach lurched. I felt sick. I pressed my hand over my mouth.

The ugly, hair-covered snout opened wide. I saw rows and rows of jagged, broken teeth.

The creature let out a bellowing roar — and shoved Mr. Fleshman again, hard against the wall.

Stunned, Mr. Fleshman hit the wall and slid to the floor.

The creature stood over him, teeth bared, skin dripping wetly off its bones.

"Get up! Get up!" I screamed without even realizing it. "Get up! Please — get up!"

My stomach lurched again. I pressed my face harder against the glass.

Mr. Fleshman climbed shakily to his feet.

He appeared dazed. Staggering, he threw out his arms — and tackled the creature around the waist.

The creature tilted back its crushed head in a loud howl as Mr. Fleshman pushed it to the floor.

They struggled. Wrestled. Out of my view.

I took a step back, my legs shaking so hard, I could barely stand. "What should I do?" I cried out loud, my voice tiny and shrill.

I peered back into the house. I couldn't see them.

Silence now.

"What should I do?"

I have to get help.

I turned. Stumbled down the porch step. Caught my balance and lurched to my house.

No one home. No one to tell.

"I'll call the police," I decided.

I glanced back at Mr. Fleshman's house. Light poured from all the windows. I couldn't see him in there. Couldn't see the hideous, one-eyed monster.

Sweat drenched my forehead, ran down my

cheeks. I squeezed through the fence. Ran as hard as I could through the back door, into the house.

Call the police. Call the police.

I dove for the phone on the kitchen counter.

But before I could pick it up, it rang.

"Huh?" I let out a startled gasp — and pressed the receiver to my ear.

"*Jack,*" a harsh voice rasped before I could say hello.

"*Jack — I'm a monster. I know you saw me. Now I have no choice. I have to come over there AND KILL YOU!*"

5

"Huh?"

The phone slid from my hand. It hit the counter and bounced onto the tile floor.

I dove for it. Grabbed it and checked to see if it had broken. Then I pressed it back against my ear.

"Who — who *is* this?" I stammered.

Silence.

The creature! Can it *talk*? I wondered.

Then I heard giggling. A girl's giggling.

Someone breathed into the phone.

"Who is it? Who's there?" I cried.

"Scared you, huh?" came the reply.

"Derek? It's *you*?"

Derek laughed. "I'm coming to get you, Jack," he whispered. "I'm right across the street."

"Get off the phone!" I cried. "This is no time for jokes! Derek — please —"

21

"Did we scare you?" I recognized Maddy's voice.

"I — I've got *real* things to be scared about!" I told her. "Maddy — please. Can you —"

"Marsha is here too," she interrupted. "And Henry. You're on the speakerphone, Jack. We heard you gasp when Derek said —"

"Can you come over?" I cried. "I'm kind of scared. I'm all alone here, Maddy. Do you think you could come over?"

She giggled. "Why?"

"I saw the monster," I told her. "I saw it. At Mr. Fleshman's house. They were fighting, and . . . and I think it *killed* Mr. Fleshman!"

I could hear them all laugh.

"Nice try, Jack," Henry said.

"We're not stupid," Derek added. "If you want to trick us, you'll have to do better than that."

"Give it a rest, Jack," I heard Marsha mutter.

"No — please!" I protested. "It's not a joke. I saw them fighting. It — it was horrible!"

"Oooh! I'm scared! I'm scared!" Henry cried.

"Get off the phone!" I screamed. "If you're not going to come over here to help me, get off the phone. I've *got* to call the police!"

"Call Dial-a-Monster!" Derek joked.

I slammed the phone down. Didn't they realize this was an emergency?

Sometimes my friends can be so lame.

My hands were shaking as I picked up the

phone again. I listened for the dial tone. Then I punched in the emergency number, 911.

It rang once.

What will I tell the police? The question forced its way into my mind. If I tell them I saw a monster next door, there's no way they'll believe me!

I'll just tell them I saw a fight, I decided. I won't mention the monster.

A second ring.

The front doorbell chimed. I slammed down the phone and spun away from the kitchen counter.

Who is at the front door?

It must be my friends, I decided. Maybe they changed their minds. Maybe they came over to see if I'm okay, to help me.

The doorbell chimed again.

"Coming!" I shouted. I took off down the hall, through the living room.

I grabbed the knob on the front door and started to turn it.

A sudden thought made me stop.

Don't open the door, I warned myself, till you know who it is.

I pulled my hand from the knob. "Who's there?" I called. My voice came out tiny and weak.

No answer.

"Who's there?" I repeated, pressing my ear against the door.

I pushed myself away from the door and ran to the living room window. Squinting out into the darkness, I saw a tall figure standing on the porch.

Mr. Fleshman!

I froze, my face pressed against the window glass. I watched Mr. Fleshman lean forward and press the doorbell again.

He's okay, I realized. He must have won that wrestling match with the creature.

But why is he here? What does he want?

The door chimes rang in my ears, startling me from my thoughts. I made my way back to the front door. I attached the chain — and opened the door a crack.

"Who is it?" I called out.

"It's Mr. Fleshman. Your neighbor," he replied. He had a hoarse, breathy voice.

"Uh . . . m-my parents aren't home," I stammered.

"That's okay," he replied, speaking softly. "I wanted to talk to you."

"What about?" I blurted out. I checked to make sure the chain was pulled tight. Then I peeked out through the crack in the doorway.

Mr. Fleshman's silver-white hair glowed in the moonlight. His face appeared calm, almost blank. He didn't look as if he'd just been in a horrible fight with a monster.

"I brought your ball back," he said, almost in a whisper. He raised the rubber ball in one hand. He held it up to the opening.

"Thanks," I replied.

I wanted to tell him to put the ball down on the porch and leave. But I knew I couldn't do that.

He held up the ball. I had no choice. I unhooked the chain and pulled open the front door. "Thanks," I repeated. I took the ball from him.

I wanted to slam the door. I wanted him to go away.

He stood so tall and straight. The silver hair made his whole head appear to glow. He narrowed his strange eyes at me.

"I know you and your friends have been spying on me, Jack," he said. He spoke slowly, and so softly, I could barely hear him. His piercing gray eyes locked coldly on mine.

"Well —" I started. My voice cracked.

"I want you to stop spying," he said through clenched teeth.

"Huh?" I let out a gasp. I didn't know what to

say. "But — I saw ... something ... in your house!" I blurted out.

"I don't care what you saw," Mr. Fleshman snapped. "My work is top secret. I can't allow you to spy on me."

"Top secret?" I said shrilly.

He didn't reply. He just stared down at me with those cold, cold eyes.

I shivered.

We stared at each other for a long while.

"Do you understand, Jack?" he said finally. "No more spying?"

I nodded.

"Good," he whispered. "Then there won't be any ... trouble ... between you and me." He leaned down, bringing his face close to mine. "You don't want trouble — *do* you?" he whispered.

He's threatening me, I realized.

I shivered again. "No. No trouble," I choked out.

He nodded, those cold eyes frozen on mine. Then he turned and strode across the front lawn to his house. He didn't glance back.

I shut the front door and locked it. Then I collapsed onto the bottom step of the front stairway. I waited for my heart to stop racing. And wiped my cold, sweaty hands on the legs of my jeans.

Now I *can't* stop spying, I told myself.

Now I have no choice. I have to find out Mr. Fleshman's secret.

He's doing something weird over there. Something he wants to hide.

If only my parents were home.

But, of course, they wouldn't believe me, anyway.

If I tell them, they'll be on Mr. Fleshman's side, I decided. They'll go to his house and apologize. They'll promise Mr. Fleshman to keep me away from his yard. Then they will punish me for bothering our neighbor.

Grownups stick together. It's really annoying.

Mr. Fleshman is hiding some kind of monster in there. A weird, evil monster. And I'm the only one who knows about it. The thought made the hairs on the back of my neck prickle. *I'm the only one.* . . .

But Mom and Dad wouldn't believe me.

Unless . . . unless I had *proof.*

I jumped to my feet.

Yes. *Proof.*

If I could show Mom and Dad some kind of evidence, some kind of *proof,* then they'd have to believe me.

I suddenly felt better. I'd made a decision. A big decision.

I knew what I had to do.

7

'm going to wait until Mr. Fleshman is away, I decided. Then I'm going to sneak into his house — and find out for myself what he is doing in there.

The next afternoon, I stood in the backyard with my binoculars to my eyes, searching the sky. It was a clear, sunny day. No clouds.

A perfect day for spying on Mr. Fleshman — and for spotting the comet.

I couldn't believe I hadn't seen it yet. On TV, the news reporters said it was big enough and bright enough to see even in daylight.

Scientists were studying it night and day. They still hadn't figured out what it was.

Sunlight glinted off the binocular lenses. I lowered the binoculars and rubbed the back of my neck. I was getting a stiff neck from staring straight up for so long!

Every few minutes, I took a quick glimpse into Mr. Fleshman's house. Nothing going on over there. His car stood in the driveway, parked half-in, half-out of the garage. But I saw no sign of him . . . or any creatures.

A shimmer of silver streaked across the sky. I grabbed for the binoculars. I pressed them to my face and stared up.

Only a distant airplane.

"Let me see!" a familiar voice demanded.

"Ow!" I let out a cry as Billie tugged the binoculars. She tugged so hard, she nearly pulled me off my feet. "They're strapped around my neck!" I cried.

"Well, take them off." She tugged them again. "It's my turn."

"Go away," I snapped. "We're not taking turns."

"I'm telling Mom!" she cried.

Doesn't she ever get tired of telling Mom?

"Get your own binoculars," I told her. "I'm not leaving this yard until I see the comet."

"I don't need your stupid binoculars," she sneered. "I already saw the comet. Actually, I saw it twice. No. Five times."

"Go away," I muttered.

To my surprise, she went away. But she stopped at the kitchen door. "You're supposed to use a telescope — not binoculars," she called.

"I don't *own* a telescope!" I shouted back.

She didn't hear me. She slammed the screen door behind her and vanished into the house.

Before I could start my search for the comet again, I saw Henry and Derek trotting around the side of the house. They both wore white, sleeveless T-shirts, and baggy shorts that came down below their knees.

"They're coming for you, Saucerman!" Derek called.

"Excuse me?" I replied.

He pointed up to the sky and grinned. "They're coming for you."

"Yeah — it's not a comet up there," Henry chimed in. "It's a UFO. They're looking for you, Saucerman. They want to take you back to your home planet!"

They both thought they were a riot. They giggled and slapped each other high- and low-fives.

"Ha-ha," I said, rolling my eyes. "Funny. Remind me to laugh."

I glanced up at the sky. Two birds sailed high above the lemon trees at the back of the yard. "What's up?" I asked.

"We're hanging out till Henry's dad gets back," Derek replied. "He's got a bunch of tickets to the Dodgers game and he's taking us. Want to come?"

I kicked at a clump of dirt. "Can't," I told them. "I've got to go with my parents to visit my cousins."

31

"Where, Saucerman?" Derek demanded. "Mars or Jupiter?"

"Burbank," I replied. "Don't call me Saucerman. Give me a break — okay?"

Henry kicked the same clump of dirt. "School starts next week. You trying out for the swim team?"

The binoculars started to feel heavy. I pulled them off and set them on the grass. "I don't know," I said. "Think I should?"

"Yeah. We need you on the team." Henry grinned, and he added, "Because you make us look good!"

They both laughed.

"That's the problem," I complained. "You guys are so much better than me, I won't even make the team."

"We'll help you," Derek offered.

"Yeah. We'll bring you floaties to wear on your arms!" Henry joked.

"Jack — ?" Mom called from the house. "Time to go!"

Henry and Derek took off. "Sorry about the Dodgers game," Henry called back. They disappeared around the side of the house.

"Dodgers game? What Dodgers game?" Mom asked.

"Never mind," I muttered.

I wasn't having a great day so far. No comet. No Dodgers game. And now I had to go spend the afternoon in Burbank with my two elderly cousins who like to pinch my cheek and tell me how big I'm growing.

Mom rubbed her hand over a stain on my Lakers T-shirt. "Is that what you're wearing, Jack? I don't think so. Go up and change your shirt, at least."

I started to protest. But a figure moving on the other side of the fence caught my eye.

Mr. Fleshman!

Mom saw him too. She raised her hand and waved to him. "Let's go say hello," Mom said.

"No. Mom —" I started to hold her back.

But she hurried over to greet him, taking long strides. I held back for a moment.

He had threatened me. He had tried to scare me.

Maybe Mom will see what a creep he is, I thought. I hurried to catch up to her.

Mr. Fleshman wore a black T-shirt and black running shorts. And he had a black baseball cap over his silver hair.

They had already introduced themselves by the time I stepped up beside Mom. "Jack has been talking about you," Mom said.

Oh, wow! I could feel the blood rushing to my face. Why did she say that?

Mr. Fleshman stared down at me with those icy gray eyes. I could see the anger in his eyes. But when he turned to Mom, a smile spread over his darkly tanned face.

"Beautiful day, isn't it?" he said cheerfully.

"Are you doing any science experiments or anything in your house?" Mom asked him.

"Science experiments?" he asked in his breathy voice.

Mom nodded. "Jack keeps telling us the strangest stories about seeing *monsters* in your house!" She laughed.

Mr. Fleshman laughed too. A cold, dry laugh that sounded more like coughing than laughing.

He glanced quickly at me. I felt a chill roll down my back.

"No. No monsters in my house," he told my mom. "No science experiments." His smile faded. "Want to know the truth?"

"Yes," Mom replied.

"I'm an alien from another planet," Mr. Fleshman said. "I keep my alien friends hidden in the house while we make our plans to take over the world."

8

"**H**e wasn't joking!" I exclaimed from the backseat of the car.

Mom turned to face me from the passenger seat in front. "Of course he was joking, Jack. What's wrong with you? Mr. Fleshman seems like a very nice man."

I sighed and adjusted my seatbelt. "Mom — how do you *know* he was joking?"

"I don't want to discuss it anymore, Jack," she replied impatiently. "I know he was joking, and so do you."

"Jack is stupid," Billie chimed in. "Jack is an alien."

"Don't call me stupid," I snapped.

"Stop it — both of you!" Dad cried. "Do you see the traffic backed up on this freeway? It's going to be a long drive. So give me a break."

I settled back in the seat and shut my eyes.

Okay, okay. I *knew* Mr. Fleshman was joking. But I also knew that he was *lying*. I saw that monster in his house, saw it *clearly* with my own eyes.

I'll get proof, I promised myself.

I'll sneak into that house and get proof.

The afternoon with my cousins was too boring to talk about. I'll only say that the two of them pinched my cheeks so hard, they changed the shape of my face!

Maybe the swelling will go down in a few days. . . .

That night, Billie, Dad, and I were in the den. Billie was watching that wildlife show again where the animals eat each other.

I was trying to show Dad how to play one of the *Mario* games on the Gameboy. But he was having a lot of trouble.

"My fingers are too big for these little controls!" Dad complained.

"Then why don't you buy me one of those Virtual Reality game players?" I suggested.

I heard Mom laugh from the living room. "Jack, you already *live* in virtual reality!" she called.

I started to reply. But another news bulletin on the TV caught my eye. Dad lowered the Gameboy to his lap, and we both stared at the screen.

"NASA scientists are still baffled by the large object circling Earth," the news reporter said.

A photo of a shimmering, round blob filled the screen.

The reporter's voice continued: "NASA still hasn't identified the object yet. But it is believed to be a large meteor."

"Wow!" Dad cried, leaning closer to the TV. "Look at that thing! That's amazing!"

"The giant meteor appears to be breaking up in our atmosphere," the reporter said. "It seems to be shooting off smaller meteors."

In the photo on the TV screen, I could see tiny dark circles flying away from the enormous, round object.

"A twenty-four-hour sky-watch has been ordered by the U.S. Air Force," the news reporter continued. "But the air force wants to assure everyone that the wild rumors about the meteor are *not* true. This is *not* a UFO. Scientists insist it is some kind of rock or mineral from deep in space."

I jumped up from the couch. "They're not telling the truth!" I cried. "I know it! It isn't a meteor. It's an alien spacecraft! Or maybe it's some kind of alien weapon! And it's *firing* at us!"

"Jack — sit down," Dad scolded. "Don't scare your sister."

I turned and saw that Billie had moved to the den window. She had pulled up the blinds and was staring out.

"Oh, wow! I see a meteorite!" she screamed,

pointing. "I see it! I see it! NOOOOOOO! *It's going to crash right into the house!*"

"Huh?" I scrambled to the window. "Where? Where?"

"I see *two* meteorites!" Billie declared. "No. *Six!*"

I stared up at the sky.

I saw the moon and a million twinkling stars.

Nothing else.

"Sit down, Billie," Dad scolded. "You scared us all. That wasn't funny."

Billie stuck out her tongue at me. "Scared *you*, Saucerman," she said, just quiet enough so that Dad couldn't hear.

I shook my head at her angrily. Why did I always fall for her dumb jokes?

"I've got to check this out!" I exclaimed.

I ran up to my room and grabbed the binoculars. Then I hurried back downstairs.

The backyard hadn't been lucky. I'd spent hours back there searching the sky until all my muscles ached. I hadn't seen a thing.

Tonight, I decided, I'll try the front yard.

As I passed the den, they were still talking on the TV about the strange meteor. I saw Billie sitting between Mom and Dad on the couch. She looked a little frightened. Dad had his arm around her. Mom held her hands.

Sometimes I get so angry at her, I forget that she's just a little kid. She pretends to be tough.

But this meteor thing must be very scary to her, I realized.

On the TV I could hear a scientist talking about the strange space object. "The public shouldn't be alarmed," I heard him say as I headed past the den. "There is certainly no reason to panic."

"Sir," a reporter asked, "do you think this space object will be with us from now on? Like a new moon or something?"

"At this point, we don't know," the scientist replied. "We can't even make a guess."

Not much of an answer, I thought. Is the government keeping something from us? I pushed open the front door and hurried outside.

It was a clear, warm night. The row of tall palm trees at the corner creaked and bent in a steady, warm breeze. A pale half-moon floated low in a sky full of twinkling stars.

I heard kids laughing and splashing in the swimming pool behind the Arthurs' house across the street. A minivan rolled by with surfboards strapped to the roof of the van, and loud country music blaring from the windows.

"Meteor — where are you?" I murmured out loud.

I raised the binoculars and began to scan the starry sky.

After a few seconds, I stopped.

I had a sudden strong feeling, a feeling that I wasn't alone. That someone was watching me.

I lowered the binoculars, turned — and saw Mr. Fleshman standing in his front yard.

Dressed all in black, he was hard to see at night. He also had binoculars raised to his eyes.

"Looking for the comet?" Mr. Fleshman asked. He didn't turn to face me. He kept his gaze on the stars. "Just waiting for my friends to land," he said.

I laughed. "You're joking — right?"

"Joking?" he replied.

He lowered his binoculars.

Turned to face me.

And I let out a *yelp* of horror as his eyeballs shot out six inches from his face!

The eyeballs bounced up and down in the darkness.

Mr. Fleshman tossed back his head and laughed a hoarse, dry laugh.

I shuddered. I felt so embarrassed.

Why did I scream like that? How could I fall for such a stupid old trick?

Plastic eyeballs on long springs. Attached to fake eyeglass frames.

So lame!

Still chuckling to himself, Mr. Fleshman pulled off the fake eyeglasses. He held them up to me. "Want to try them?"

"Uh . . . no thanks," I choked out. I felt like such a total jerk for screaming.

"I made them," he said, still holding them out to me. "They're pretty real-looking, huh?"

"I guess," I replied.

Why did he pull that joke on me? I wondered. Was he waiting for me out here? Was he suddenly trying to be friendly? Or did he want to scare me?

"Have you seen the meteor?" I asked, gazing up at the sky.

Mr. Fleshman shook his head. He crossed the lawn and stopped a few inches from me. "I don't think it's in our hemisphere now," he said. "I don't think it will orbit over us until tomorrow."

"Do you think it's a comet or a meteor — or what?" I asked.

He didn't answer. He studied me with those strange gray eyes.

"My sister Billie is scared of it," I continued. "She thinks it's some kind of spaceship or something."

My mouth suddenly felt dry. I realized I was talking rapidly. Talking a lot. Because I was nervous.

Mr. Fleshman didn't say anything. His smile faded as his eyes locked on mine.

"You talk a lot to your mother, don't you, Jack?" he asked. His cold, hoarse voice sent a shiver down my back.

"Excuse me?" I blurted out.

"You've been telling your mother things?" he rasped. He leaned over me. So tall. Those eyes so frozen, so . . . evil.

42

"Uh . . . I . . ."

"You've been telling her stories . . . about me?" he demanded.

I took a deep breath. "I — I told you," I stammered. "I saw a creature. In your house. I saw you fighting. I —"

He loomed over me. In the moonlight, his silver hair glowed as if electric. He clenched his jaw. I could see the vein in his neck pulsing.

"I . . . don't . . . like . . . people . . . telling . . . stories . . . about . . . me, Jack," he said slowly, through gritted teeth. "I . . . don't . . . like . . . it . . . at . . . all."

I opened my mouth to reply. But only a frightened squeak came out.

My heart pounded. My knees started to buckle. I felt like I was going to faint or something.

Somehow I stayed on my feet. "Sorry," I choked out. Then I turned and started to run back to my house.

"Your last warning, Jack!" he called after me. "That was it — your last warning!"

I flew into the house. And slammed the door shut behind me.

I stood in the front hall, shaking, struggling to catch my breath.

He can't do that to me! I decided. He can't frighten me away like that.

He's hiding something in his house — and I'm

going to find out what it is. I'm going to get my proof, I promised myself! He can't scare me away.

The next morning, I kept my promise.

The next morning, I sneaked into his house.

And I found my proof.

10

Morning sunlight streamed through the kitchen window. Birds chirped from the lemon trees in the backyard. I sat on a stool at the kitchen counter and gulped down my Frosted Flakes.

"Why are you eating that so fast?" Mom asked, leaning against the counter.

"I always eat cereal this fast," I told her. "I don't like it to get soggy."

She brushed back my hair. "Makes sense," she said. She crossed the kitchen to the coffeemaker and poured herself a mug of coffee.

I gulped down the rest. Raised the bowl to my mouth. Slurped up the milk.

Then I hurried outside to check for the meteor.

The sun was so bright, the whole yard glowed. I

45

squinted up into the sky. Wisps of white clouds sailed overhead.

And what was that white dot?

A pale white dot, floating low, under the clouds. Was that it? Was that the meteor?

"Wow!" I let out an excited cry. I had to get my binoculars. Finally! The meteor was flying into view.

I couldn't take my eyes off it. I squinted up at it, a tiny white speck, moving slowly under the wispy clouds.

Would the binoculars make it clearer? I started to turn back to the house. But I saw something move in Mr. Fleshman's kitchen window.

And I gasped.

I saw the crushed skull. The dangling eye.

The creature.

I squinted into the window, shielding my eyes with one hand. I took a few steps toward the fence. The creature didn't move.

Sunlight reflecting on the windowpane made it impossible to see clearly. I squeezed through the opening in the fence, into Mr. Fleshman's yard.

I squinted into the window again. Gone. The creature was gone.

Had it been there in the first place? Or was the bright sunlight playing tricks with my eyes?

The garage door stood open, I saw. The garage was empty. No sign of the little black convertible.

I saw the morning newspaper lying near the

street. Mr. Fleshman always picked up his newspaper first thing every morning.

He's away, I decided. Maybe he went away for the weekend.

My chance to explore the house. My chance to find my proof.

Was I brave enough?

Maybe.

My heart started to pound. I peered through the window in the door. No one in the kitchen.

No human. And no creature.

Should I knock?

If Mr. Fleshman is home and he comes to the door, what do I say?

I'll tell him I'm sorry I spied on him, I decided.

I knocked on the kitchen door. Three sharp raps. "Anyone home?" I called.

Silence.

I grabbed the knob. "He's not home," I said out loud. "I'm going in."

The door was locked. But the kitchen window was open. I lifted myself over the window ledge and slid inside.

I tiptoed into the kitchen. It smelled kind of peppery. Spicy. I checked out the counter and the sink. No breakfast dishes. Everything clean and put away.

Mr. Fleshman must have left last night, I decided.

I took a deep breath and started toward the

back hall. Am I really doing this? I asked myself. Am I really sneaking around in someone else's house?

Too late to wimp out now, Jack, I scolded myself. You're already here — aren't you?

Walking silently, I took a few steps into the hall. "Uh . . . anyone home?" I called in a tiny voice. "Mr. Fleshman?"

No reply.

The sunlight ended in the kitchen. The long hall stood in deep shadow. I took another few steps, my eyes darting back and forth.

Two huge eyes stared out at me from the wall. I stopped and stared back. A large poster. A movie poster. EYES OF THE MONSTER, it proclaimed in dripping red letters. GAZE INTO ITS EYES AND DIE A THOUSAND DEATHS!

"Whoa," I murmured.

The walls were covered with old movie posters. FANGS OF THE PHANTOM, the next one read. Across the hall, a tattered mummy reached a half-decayed hand toward me. THE MUMMY'S GRASP.

"Cool!" I murmured. Mr. Fleshman had the greatest collection of horror movie posters! They were framed and lined up one after the other down the long hall.

Where did he get these? I wondered. I'm really into old horror movies. But I hadn't even *heard* of these movies.

I had my eyes on the posters, so I didn't see the
little table against the wall. I bumped it hard with
my knee. "Ow!" I cried out as pain shot up my leg.

I stumbled over the table. Grabbed the wall to
keep from falling.

A large book fell off the table. It slammed noisily against the floor.

I waited for a moment, catching my breath,
waiting for my knee to stop throbbing. Then I
bent to pick up the book.

It wasn't a book, I realized. It was a photo
album.

The pages were open. I dropped to my knees
and gazed at the color snapshots.

"Huh?" A startled gasp escaped my throat.
"Weird," I murmured.

The photos ... they were all snapshots of ugly
green creatures.

The creatures were shaped like humans. They
had very smooth, very shiny green heads. And
oval black eyes — solid black eyes, like big black
olives. Two nostrils in the center of their head,
right below the eyes. No noses. Just nostrils.

Their long green arms looked more like plant
tendrils than arms. The arms ended in slender,
three-fingered hands.

"What *is* this?" I murmured. I flipped through

the thick photo album. Page after page of snap-shots of these creatures.

Are they models? I wondered. Are they some kind of dummies or display mannequins?

Each one looked slightly different. They were all slender and shiny and green. But some crea-tures were tall, and some were short. Some had big, oval black eyes. Some had smaller eyes and bigger nostrils.

One creature had a row of orange sticks popping up from the top of its head. Some kind of weird hairstyle? Another creature had the sticks poking out from where its chin should be.

"Weird," I kept murmuring as I flipped through the pages. "Weird . . ."

What *are* these creatures? I wondered. Are they real? Are they alive?

Have I found the proof I need? If I take this to my parents, will they finally believe me about Mr. Fleshman?

I closed the photo album and tucked it under my arm. I'm not really *stealing* it, I told myself. I'm just borrowing it for a short while.

I'll return it after I've proven to Mom and Dad that Mr. Fleshman is weird. That he's doing some-thing very strange in this house.

Holding on to the album, I started to turn back to the kitchen. But gray light flooding from a room across the hall caught my eye.

I peeked into the room — and let out a cry.

The photo album slid out from under my arm and dropped to the floor.

I stared at the long black box in the center of the room.

A coffin.

I'd seen plenty of coffins in horror movies. But I'd never seen one in real life.

Its shiny black wood glowed in the eerie gray light. The lid was closed. Two brass handles glimmered dully on the side.

I glanced quickly around the small room. Dark drapes covered the window. A tall, wooden dresser rested against one wall. A straight-backed, wooden chair stood next to the dresser.

No other furniture.

Just a long black coffin in the center of the room.

I took a few steps into the room. The dark wood of the coffin was so shiny, I could see my reflection in the side.

"Whoa." I stopped when I heard the soft creaking sound.

Was that a door opening? A footstep?

I heard it again. *CREEEEEAK. CREEE-EEAK.*

I froze. My heart stopped.

The coffin lid — it was sliding open!

"Noooo!" A hoarse cry escaped my throat.

I didn't wait to see who — or what — came climbing out of that coffin.

I flew from the room and slammed the door shut behind me.

I ran down the hall, past the posters of staggering mummies and roaring monsters.

Into another room. Not the kitchen. I'd run the wrong way.

I had stumbled into some kind of workshop or lab.

Over my panting breath, I heard a bubbling sound. A long table held test tubes and beakers. Tangles of wires and tubes stretched along the low ceiling. Strange, electronic machines lined the walls.

Red and blue lights flickered and flashed. A

bubbly blue liquid frothed over the sides of a huge glass jar.

What *is* this stuff? I asked myself, my eyes flashing from one thing to another, struggling to take it all in. What on earth does Mr. Fleshman do in here?

If he went away, why didn't he shut this stuff off? Why did he leave it all going?

I didn't have time to think up any answers for any of my questions.

I heard a hissing sound, like air escaping from a tire.

I felt a wash of cold air.

Turning toward the sound, I saw a thick mist rising up from behind the lab table. Like a cloud, it floated up into the room.

And as it floated, it took shape.

A billowy head formed on top of puffy white shoulders.

The head folded in on itself. Shifted. Folded again.

I saw two gray eyes. A misty mouth.

The mouth opened in a horrifying moan. Human and not human.

"Ooooooohhhhhhhh."

The figure floated higher. Growing as it floated toward me.

A ghost! A real ghost.

The misty figure floated over me.

Spread itself, darkening, darkening.

Covering me in its icy chill.

12

"**O**oooohhhh.**" Another low moan.
The eerie sound vibrated all around me.

The ghost rolled over me.

I let out a frightened cry.

It swept around me like a cold mist. Swirling, swirling.

Alive.

With a sharp gasp, I ducked under it.

Then I burst forward. I hit the lab table. Several beakers and tubes crashed to the tabletop. A thick blue liquid puddled onto the floor.

I spun to the door.

And stumbled to the hall. Dark and quiet out here.

In the room behind me, I heard another low moan from the misty ghost.

"What is going *on* here?" I screamed out loud.

I staggered back as a figure appeared at the end of the hallway.

The creature!

It turned toward me, hunched its decaying shoulders, and grunted, nodding its ugly head as if it recognized me.

It took a heavy step toward me.

Then another.

I gaped in horror at its sick, dripping flesh, its dangling eye, the broken teeth, so yellow against the green, crushed face.

It grunted again. And snapped its jaws hungrily.

Oh, wow. I was right about Mr. Fleshman.

The whole time, I was right.

I *knew* something horrible was going on in here. Why didn't anyone believe me?

Now it was too late. Too late . . .

Unless I found a way out.

THUD. . . . THUD.

The creature lumbered heavily toward me.

I ducked back into the lab. I had nowhere else to go.

I glanced frantically around the terrifying room, searching for a weapon. Something to throw at the creature. Something to slow it down so I could escape.

Escape . . .

I grabbed the first thing I could find. A small, square object. Metal.

I'll aim for its head, I told myself. I squeezed the object tightly in my palm.

My legs trembled.

THUD . . . THUD.

My whole body shook with each footstep.

Hit it in the head — and run, I instructed myself. Then run back through the kitchen.

Get home. Get home. Get home.

I forced myself into the hall.

The huge creature stood a few feet away, blocking my path. Its eye dangled. It uttered low grunts. It took a heavy step closer.

I raised the metal square. Prepared to heave it.

And felt a hand on my shoulder.

I screamed. Spun around.

And stared up into the grinning face of Mr. Fleshman.

"I warned you, Jack," he whispered. "You should have listened."

is hand tightened on my shoulder.

"I — I — I — " I sputtered.

His grin grew wider. "Jack, you're *shaking*!" he exclaimed.

"I'm sorry," I said. "I didn't know. I mean, I didn't see anything. Really! I won't tell anyone! Please — "

He snickered.

"No, I swear!" I cried. "Please let me go! I won't tell anyone what I saw!"

"Well, I hope not," he said, letting go of my shoulder. "If you told, it could cost me my job."

"Huh? Job?" My voice broke. I leaned back against the wall and struggled to stop my legs from trembling.

Mr. Fleshman nodded. "I design special effects," he explained, "for horror movies."

I stared at him. I opened my mouth to say something, but no sound came out.

He rested a hand on the furry green shoulder of the creature. "Like my guy here? I call him Cutey. Because he's so cute." He pinched the creature's long snout.

"You — you made him?" I stammered.

Mr. Fleshman nodded again. "Yeah. I made him. He's radio-controlled."

He held up a little remote controller, like a TV remote. He pushed a button, and the creature's snout opened and closed. He pressed another button, and the eyes blinked.

"Wow! That's awesome!" I exclaimed. I was starting to feel a little more normal. I realized I owed Mr. Fleshman an apology. "I'm sorry I sneaked into your house," I started.

He held up a hand. "Don't apologize," he said. "I set this all up for you. I put Cutey in the kitchen window to get your attention. I saw you come in. I was waiting."

"But — why?" I demanded. "First you tried to scare me away. Then —"

"My work is top secret," Mr. Fleshman replied, leaning on Cutey. "I tried to stop you from spying on me. But I could see that you weren't going to stop. So I decided to give you a good scare instead."

"Well, you scared me!" I confessed.

"Did you like my ghost effect?" Mr. Fleshman asked. He led the way back into the lab.

"How did you make the mist do that?" I asked.

"It's a projection. See?" He pulled out an electronic box that looked like a VCR. He pressed a button, and light poured from a small lens.

"I project the ghost over the room," Mr. Fleshman explained.

I watched the mist begin to form again. It looked so real!

"It's pretty simple, actually. Everything you saw, Jack, is special effects. But I can't have anyone spying on me and learning my tricks."

I apologized again.

Then he apologized to me. "Hope I didn't scare you too badly. Sometimes I get a little carried away." He laughed. "What did you think was going on in here?"

"I'm not really sure," I told him. "I saw you wrestling with Cutey, and —"

"I was testing him out," Mr. Fleshman explained.

"Well, I won't tell anyone about what I saw," I promised. I followed him to the kitchen door. I started to go out — but then I remembered something.

"The photo album," I said.

He narrowed his silver-gray eyes at me. "What's that?"

"I saw that photo album," I told him. "With all the green creatures in it. What was that?"

He sighed. "Those were model creatures I built for a movie. I must have made a hundred different ones. What a shame. The film never came out."

"Do you still have the models?" I asked.

He shook his head. "No. The movie studio owned them. And the studio went out of business."

I stepped onto the back stoop. "Well, thanks for the horror show," I said. "I promise I'll never spy on you again, Mr. Fleshman."

He laughed. "Maybe I'll use you as a tester, Jack. You know. Try out some of my new creations on you."

"Wow. That would be awesome!" I cried. I said good-bye and hurried home.

I couldn't wait to tell Mom and Dad that I was wrong about Mr. Fleshman. That he really was a nice guy. I knew they would tease me and say, "I told you so." But I didn't care.

I felt so relieved, so happy to know the truth about my neighbor and what went on in his house.

I had no way of knowing that the scary part of my life was just beginning.

ell, I'm glad you solved that mystery," Mom said at dinner. She passed the bucket of chicken. My favorite — extra crispy. "So Mr. Fleshman works in horror movies."

"I knew that," Billie chimed in. She had mashed potato gravy all over her chin. "I knew all those scary things were special effects."

"You did not!" I snapped.

"Did too!"

"Did not! No way!"

"Could we have a quiet dinner for once?" Dad sighed. He told Billie to wipe her chin. Then he lowered a forkful of mashed potatoes and turned to me. "So the mystery is solved? No more wild stories?"

"No more wild stories," I promised.

"Jack can't help it," Billie sneered. "He *has* to tell wild stories."

"Do not!" I cried. "It's just that —"

"Ask him why everyone calls him Saucerman," Billie said to Mom and Dad. "Go ahead. Ask him."

"Shut up, Billie," I whispered.

"Why *do* they call you Saucerman?" Mom asked.

I shrugged. "Beats me."

The next few days flew past quickly. The last days of summer vacation always go much too fast!

I had two Summer Reading books to read. I made it through the first one and half of the second.

When I didn't have my face buried in a book, I was scanning the skies, searching for the meteor. It was the biggest story on all the TV news shows.

The silvery object just kept circling Earth — and scientists around the world were still puzzled by it.

None of them could agree about what it was or where it came from!

I searched and searched. But I never spotted it.

Sunday night before the first day of school, I forgot about the meteor. I could only think about school. Who would be my teacher? Who would be in my class?

Getting undressed for bed, I felt something in my jeans pocket. I reached inside and pulled out the square, metal object from Mr. Fleshman's lab.

I must have jammed it into my pocket that day in Mr. Fleshman's house, I realized. I turned it in my hand and examined it.

It was shiny and black, about the size of a beeper.

Why did I ever think this would make a good weapon against that big monster? I wondered. In my panic, I wasn't thinking clearly.

The little square felt smooth all around. I pressed a small black button on the back, but nothing happened. Holding it close, I saw tiny holes across the top. Three rows of them.

Maybe it's a high-tech saltshaker, I thought.

I didn't mean to take it. I'll return it to Mr. Fleshman tomorrow, I told myself. I set it down on my dresser top and went to bed.

It took a long while to fall asleep. I thought about school. And I kept thinking about everything I'd seen at Mr. Fleshman's house that day. The awesome movie posters . . . the ghost projection . . . the radio-controlled monster . . .

Then, half-awake, half-asleep, I heard voices.

Tinny voices, as if from far away. Funny, high voices like Munchkins from *The Wizard of Oz*. Talking rapidly. All talking at once.

Was I dreaming? Was someone talking in the backyard?

I struggled to hear what they were saying. But

the voices slipped under the hiss and whistle of static, like a distant radio station fading in, then fading out.

The static rose and fell. The voices jabbered on, like music.

What were they saying? Was someone talking to me?

Was someone trying to wake me up? Or was it all part of a dream? Such a frustrating dream. I really wanted to know what they were saying.

I tossed and turned all night. I turned my head to one side, then the other. But the voices stayed in my ear. Tinny, almost metallic voices, falling and rising over the hissing static.

I buried my head in the pillow. I pulled the pillow over my head and pressed it over my ears.

But the voices stayed. Talking so fast, so excitedly.

They didn't stop until Mom's voice awakened me with a start. "Jack! Jack!" she called from outside my bedroom door. "Time to wake up! School!"

I sat straight up. Wide awake.

I climbed to my feet and stood stiffly.

"Jack? Do you hear me?" Mom called in. "Time to wake up for school."

"I am ready," I declared in a loud, clear voice. "I will obey!"

hat?" Mom called through the door. "What did you say?"

I realized I was standing at attention, standing so stiffly in the center of my room. "I am ready!" I repeated, shouting the words as if I were a soldier. "I will obey!"

"Stop clowning around," Mom said. "Just get dressed. Your sister is already downstairs."

I stood in place, listening to her make her way down the stairs. Then I forced my body to relax.

"Why did I say that?" I asked myself out loud.

I glanced around the room. Everything appeared the same. But I felt different. I felt . . . confused.

I heard a buzzing in my head. A chirping, like a million crickets. I shook my head. Tried to clean out my ears with my fingers.

But the soft chirping was coming from somewhere else.

I started to pull on a fresh pair of jeans. A voice whispered to me. Two voices. Three. From somewhere nearby.

The voices sounded like the chirp of insects. *But I understood them!*

"When are you coming?" I asked them. "Can you tell me what day?"

I listened to their tinny, distant reply.

And then I saluted like a soldier. "I will be prepared!" I announced to them.

I stared at the square, black box on my dresser top. The voices chirped from the box. Several voices at once.

I picked up the box. I could feel it vibrate as the voices buzzed.

"What do you want me to do?" I called into the box. "When are you coming?"

And then I gasped.

Who are they? Why am I talking to them? Why can I understand them? What do they want from me?

A million questions flashed into my mind. A million frightening questions.

I grabbed the box and tucked it into my jeans pocket.

I have to return it, I told myself, shaking in fear.

The voices are doing something to me. The voices are making me act funny.

I can't make them stop. I have to return the box to Mr. Fleshman.

Mr. Fleshman . . .

Was this some kind of movie special effect?

If it was just a movie trick, why was it making me act so strange?

I pulled on a T-shirt over the jeans and quickly slipped into socks and sneakers. Then I ran downstairs, through the kitchen to the back door.

"Where do you think you're going?" Mom asked. She sat across from Billie at the counter. Billie was spooning up big globs of cereal.

"I have to return something," I said, pulling open the door.

"Not until you've had breakfast," Mom said sharply. She pointed to the stool. "Sit."

The voices chirped in my ears.

"I will obey," I said.

I turned and made my way to the counter. I plopped onto the stool across from Billie. "Jack," Billie said, "I'll bet you get Mr. Laker." She laughed. Mr. Laker was the hardest, strictest teacher in the school.

Billie said something else, but I didn't hear her. The voices drowned her out.

"Jack — is your backpack all packed up?" Mom asked. She crossed the room to get more coffee.

"I will be prepared," I said.

Billie was still talking about Mr. Laker. But the

voices rose in my ears. I saw Billie's lips move, but I couldn't hear her.

"Stop it! Stop it!" I screamed.

"I didn't do anything!" Billie wailed.

"Leave me alone!" I told the voices.

"I *am* leaving you alone!" Billie shrieked.

"Jack — what is your problem?" Mom demanded sternly.

My head cleared. I stared up at her.

"Why are you yelling at your sister like that?" Mom asked, leaning over me.

"I — I don't know," I muttered. "I can't help it." The voices started chirping again.

"Mom — tell him to stop staring at me!" Billie whined. "Jack is trying to scare me."

"Jack, shape up," Mom scolded. "Aren't you excited about the first day of school?"

"I will be prepared," I said.

"Stop talking like a robot," Mom ordered. "You're scaring your sister." And then she added, "You're scaring me too."

"I will obey," I replied.

I shut my eyes and tried to push away the voices. I knew what I had to do. I had to return the little box to Mr. Fleshman.

I jumped up. Grabbed my backpack. And ran out the back door.

I heard Mom calling after me. But I didn't stop.

I was desperate to return the black box to Mr. Fleshman.

I had the box in my hand. I started up his drive-way.

But the voices . . . the voices . . .

They ordered me to turn around. Chattering so loudly in my ears, they ordered me away.

I tried to fight them.

I took a few steps up the driveway. I waved the box in the air, in case Mr. Fleshman was watching from the front window.

But a sharp pain shot through my head. My temples ached. I saw a bright flash of white.

Hot, white pain.

I turned and ran. Ran all the way to school. Ran with the little box in my hand, the voices chatter-ing in my ears.

School went okay — for a while. I didn't get Mr. Laker for homeroom. I got Mrs. Hoff, who is supposed to be really nice. And my friends were all in my class.

I tucked the little box deep in my backpack. I didn't hear the voices all morning. I didn't hear them again — until art class.

Mrs. Hansen, the art teacher, reminded me of a buzzing bee. She's short and round and bounces from table to table in the art room.

She announced that we'd spend our first day doing clay portraits. She asked Maddy to be our model. Maddy pretended to be shy as she took her place on a high stool in front of the art room.

But we all know that Maddy isn't shy about anything.

She struck a movie-star pose. She sat perfectly so that the sunlight from the art room window slanted across her face and lit up her hair.

I started with Maddy's legs. I know it's weird, but I like to start with the legs and then work up to the face. The clay felt soft and warm in my hands. I started to relax and enjoy working with it.

I molded Maddy's left leg. Then I started on the right leg, working the clay off the body.

I wanted to think while the voices were silent. While I could think clearly without their droning, insect chirps blocking off my thoughts.

What is this box? I asked myself. And why was it in Mr. Fleshman's house? And why does it have power over me?

Did Mr. Fleshman lie to me? Is it possible that he *isn't* a special-effects man for the movies?

If he isn't . . . what *is* he?

Static whistled through my mind. I set down my sculpture and shut my eyes.

The voices were back. Chirping and chattering. Talking to me. Filling my brain. Filling it. Filling it . . .

"Jack — what do you call this?" Mrs. Hansen's voice broke through the chirping, the whistling, the static.

I opened my eyes.

Mrs. Hansen picked up my sculpture and held it up for everyone to see. I gasped as I saw what I had molded.

A ball. A perfect, round ball.

"What is this?" Mrs. Hansen demanded.

"It's his brain!" Maddy exclaimed nastily from the front of the room.

"Saucerman strikes again!" I heard Henry declare.

"I am ready!" I shouted, jumping to my feet. "I will obey!" I saluted. Then I took the clay ball from Mrs. Hansen and heaved it across the room.

It smacked hard against a window. The pane shuddered but didn't break. The ball stuck to the glass.

Mrs. Hansen let out a startled cry.

Some kids laughed. Others grew silent.

"Why did you do that, Jack?" Mrs. Hansen demanded, narrowing her eyes at me. "I don't think that is funny."

"I am ready," I repeated, speaking from my robotlike trance. "They are coming!"

"Stop that, Jack," Mrs. Hansen scolded. "You're scaring everyone. Why did you throw that clay?"

"Huh?" Voices buzzed in my ear. I could barely hear my own voice.

"The others are coming. From their planet," I announced. "They are coming very soon."

The teacher's hand tightened on my shoulder. She turned me toward the door and gave me a gentle push. "Class," she said loudly, "I'll be back in a minute."

Everyone stared at me as she guided me out into the hall.

I swallowed hard, trying to choke down my fear. "Where are you taking me?" I cried. "Where?"

"So then, what happened at the nurse's office?" Mom asked.

I stared down at the two hot dogs on my dinner plate. I love hot dogs. I always wish we could have hot dogs for dinner *every* night.

But tonight, my stomach felt like a rock. I didn't think I could choke down a bite.

"So? What did the nurse say to you, Jack?" Dad asked impatiently.

Billie stared across the table at me, shoving nearly a whole hot dog into her mouth, chewing hard.

"Not much," I replied. "She asked me a bunch of questions. Then she made me take a nap on a cot in the back. I was totally embarrassed. When I came out, just about every kid in school made fun of me. Kids I didn't even know!"

"Never mind that," Mom said, frowning. "What kinds of questions did she ask you?"

I lowered my head. I kicked the table leg. I didn't really want to talk about this. "Just questions," I muttered. "About the meteor. Whatever."

"Huh?" Dad let his forkful of potato salad fall to his plate. "What about the meteor?"

"The nurse asked me if I was frightened by it," I told him. "She asked me if all the news reports on TV had scared me. She said maybe that's why I was acting strange."

Mom and Dad both stared at me. I guess they were expecting me to say more. Billie burped.

I stared back at them.

"Are you scared?" Mom asked finally.

I nodded. "Yes. I'm scared."

I decided to show them why. I pulled the little black box from my pocket and set it down on the table.

"What's that?" Dad asked.

"Where did you get that?" Mom asked.

"From Mr. Fleshman's house," I told them. "There are voices in it. Strange voices. They're silent now. But they talk to me. They —"

Dad reached across the table and picked it up. "It's a beeper," he said, turning it over in his hands.

"No —!" I protested. "The voices come through it. From outer space, I think. I can understand them. They talk to me."

Billie laughed.

Mom told her to hush up.

Dad studied the black box. He passed it to Mom. "It's just an ordinary beeper, Jack," he said. "You can't hear voices in it."

"But I *do!*" I cried. "They tell me what to do. And they —"

"Why did Mr. Fleshman give you this?" Mom demanded suspiciously.

"He — he didn't," I stammered. "I took it."

"Then you have to give it right back," she said sternly.

"I know," I said. "I *want* to give it back. The voices —"

"Why do you keep talking about voices?" Dad demanded.

"I hear them!" Billie cried. "This time, they're talking to *me* — not Jack!"

"Shut up, Billie!" I screamed. I could feel myself losing it, but I didn't care. "Shut up! Shut up! Shut up!"

I desperately wanted my parents to believe me. And I knew they never would if Billie started her dumb games.

"Stop screaming at your sister," Mom snapped.

"I don't hear anything," Dad said. He held the box to his ear and listened for a long while. Then he lowered the box and shook his head. "No. Not a sound."

"But — but —" I grabbed it back. "The

voices — they're quiet now. But they've been telling me things. Telling me about the visitors. They're coming. You've got to believe me. They're coming real soon!"

By the time I finished that speech, I was panting like a dog. But at least I got it all out.

Did they believe me?

Mom and Dad exchanged glances. "This is pretty serious," Mom said softly. "Jack, I think we should take you to see Dr. Bendix."

"Take me too!" Billie protested. She jumped up from her chair. "Take *me* to the doctor. I've been acting strange too! I hear voices too! Take me!"

"Sit down," Dad told her sharply.

"Do you see what a bad effect this is having on Billie?" Mom asked.

"I don't *care* about Billie!" I shrieked. "Why won't you believe me? Why?"

I didn't wait for an answer.

I grabbed the black box. Shoved back my chair. Dove away from the table. And took off out the back door.

I had to get this thing back to Mr. Fleshman. I had to return it before I went totally *crazy*!

And I had to find out the truth. What was it? Why did Mr. Fleshman have it? He was lying about being a special-effects man. He had to be.

But, then, what was he? Why were these strange voices trying to talk to him? Where were the voices coming from?

I needed answers — and I needed them right away.

My parents thought I was going crazy. Everyone at school thought I was crazy.

Only Mr. Fleshman could set the record straight.

It had rained that afternoon. My sneakers slid over the wet grass. The fence boards felt wet and cold as I slipped through the opening and made my way into Mr. Fleshman's backyard.

I went a few steps — and stumbled over something big and alive. The creature cried out in surprise. Then it backed away from me, wagging its tail.

"Bruiser?"

I recognized our neighbor's black Lab from down the block.

"You scared me, boy," I told the dog. I reached down to pet its head — but my hand stopped in midair.

I stared at the object tucked between its jaws.

A ball. Just an ordinary tennis ball.

Why did it frighten me so much? Why did that ball make me want to scream? And scream and scream?

"Go home," I ordered the dog. "Go home, boy. Go!"

I stepped around the dog. And made my way to the back porch.

I gasped when I saw Mr. Fleshman. He stood in

the kitchen doorway. In the light from the kitchen, his silvery hair glowed eerily. His gray eyes froze on mine. A strange smile spread slowly over his face.

"Jack," he said in his whispery voice, "I've been expecting you."

17

"Huh?" I let out a gasp.

Those silvery metal eyes. They seemed to be staring right through me. Icy cold, they sent chill after chill rolling down my back.

"Why did you expect me?" I managed to choke out.

His smile grew wider. He shrugged. "I thought you'd probably like to see more movie magic," he said.

He leaned down, bringing his face close to mine. "Now that you know my secret," he whispered, "I expect you want to see some more movie tricks."

I pulled back. "No — !" I cried, louder than I had planned. I couldn't hide the panic from my voice.

I held up the little black box. "I — I found this,"

I stammered. "I mean, I took it by mistake. I didn't mean to take it, but —"

He waved his hand as if to say, *No problem.*

I held it out to him. I waited for the voices to try to stop me.

But Mr. Fleshman grabbed the box from my trembling hand.

"You found my beeper?" he said, twirling it in his fingers. "That's great. I've been looking all over for it." He slid it into the pocket of his khakis.

"Beeper?" I cried. "No! It's not a beeper. I mean —"

He pulled it out of his pocket and held it up again. "Yes, it's a beeper," he said, eyeing me suspiciously. "I bought it so the movie studio can contact me when I'm not home."

"But I heard voices —" I started.

He narrowed those eerie, chrome eyes at me. "Voices?"

"Yes. Funny voices."

He held it up to his ear. "Voices?" He laughed. "You didn't hear any voices from this little thing, Jack. It beeps when I have a phone message. That's all."

I stared hard at him, studying his eyes, studying his face. Was he telling the truth? He appeared totally serious.

But what did that mean? Did that mean I really was losing it? I really was going crazy?

Mr. Fleshman held open the screen door. "Come on in," he offered. "I'll show you what I'm working on. I think you'll like it."

"Uh . . . no," I replied, taking a step back. "I can't. I —"

"It's a model of a two-headed shark," Mr. Fleshman continued. "The heads move independently. And each mouth opens and closes by a different controller. I'm having trouble with the body. I've got to hide a lot of electrical stuff in the body. And it makes it too wide. But —"

"I really can't see it now," I interrupted. "Thanks. But I have to get back. I just wanted to return the . . . beeper."

He nodded. "Okay. Some other time. See you, Jack." He headed into the house.

I started to walk back to my house. My head buzzed as if it were filled with a thousand swarming bees. I felt so confused. So worried and upset.

I need time to think about this, I decided. I can't just go home. Maybe I'll get my bike and take a long ride. Try to figure out what is happening to me. Or maybe I'll just walk.

I turned at Mr. Fleshman's driveway and made my way toward the street. I saw Bruiser, the big black Lab, loping home, the ball still tucked in his mouth.

I glanced up at my house. The front windows

were dark. I guessed that Mom, Dad, and Billie were still in back in the dining room.

They think I'm crazy, I thought sadly.

And now, I know that they're probably right.

A beeper. It was just a stupid beeper.

I kicked a jagged chunk of curb pavement out of my path. It skidded over the street.

I felt like kicking things. I felt like screaming and punching and kicking. I felt like opening my mouth in a deafening roar and tearing across the front lawns like a wild animal.

But, instead, I kicked the chunk of pavement again. This time, it crumbled in half. I lowered my head and started to walk, thinking hard, thinking about everything that had happened.

At first, I ignored the shrill whistling sound overhead. I heard it faintly, somewhere in the background of my thoughts.

But the whistle grew louder. So loud, I could no longer ignore it.

I glanced up to see where it was coming from.

And saw a blazing orange ball in the night sky.

A ball?

Whirling down, down, down . . . fiery red and yellow sparks shot off from all sides of it.

Like fireworks, I thought.

And then I didn't have time to think of anything else.

Because the big fireball plunged down on top of me.

Its light — so blinding white — so blinding —
so bright — swept around me. Swallowing me.
And I died, screaming.
Screaming.
Screaming.

 shattering *THUD* drowned out my screams.

Then, silence.

I opened my eyes to find myself on my knees in the grass.

Alive. I was alive!

The blinding light had vanished. I knelt in a puddle of light from the street lamp.

My throat ached from screaming. My heart pounded.

I took a deep breath. The air suddenly had a salty, sour smell. Like being near the ocean.

As my eyes adjusted, I saw dozens of sparkling dots, like fireflies. Squinting, I saw that they were embers. Burning pieces of rock, making the street and sidewalk sparkle.

Unreal.

I stared in disbelief, watching the embers burn, sizzling and smoking until they faded to nothing.

And then I saw the orange ball. Glowing dully. The fireball from the sky.

It had landed at the bottom of Mr. Fleshman's driveway.

So close, I realized. It had dropped so close to me.

I started to shake. My teeth chattered.

I tried to climb off my knees. But I was trembling too hard.

Staring at the orange ball, I waited until my heart stopped racing. Then, slowly, I pulled myself to my feet.

I walked over to the glowing, orange ball.

A meteorite!

"I don't *believe* this!" I murmured out loud.

I saw an actual meteorite fall. It almost fell *on top of me*!

Unbelievable! Unreal!

Awesome!

I didn't have words for it. I didn't know what to say. What to *think*!

And now I stood over it, staring down at it, unable to stop trembling. From fright? From amazement?

A perfectly round ball of rock. A rock from outer space!

How many millions of miles had it traveled to

Earth? Millions and millions of miles — and it fell just *feet* away from me!

I leaned over it, propping my hands on my knees. The air around it felt hot. And the sour, fishy aroma grew stronger.

As I stared down, the orange glow faded ... faded ... and went out.

How hot is it? I wondered.

Can I pick it up?

The rock was about the size of a croquet ball. Lowering my face just inches above it, I discovered that it wasn't perfectly smooth. Tiny craters dotted the surface all around.

I can't believe I'm staring at a rock from outer space! I told myself.

I couldn't hold back. I had to touch it.

But what if it was burning hot?

I searched the ground and picked up a long twig. I steadied my trembling hand by using *both* hands. And pressed the twig against the meteorite.

It didn't sizzle or smoke.

I felt the tip of the twig. Warm, but not really hot. I tossed the twig away. And knelt down beside the rock.

Could I touch it? Did I dare?

I had to.

I stuck out my pointer finger. Lowered it ... lowered it.

And gave the meteorite the lightest, tenth-of-a-second touch.

I jerked my hand back. Waited for the burning pain.

None.

I pushed my finger forward again. And pressed it onto the rough surface of the rock. This time, I left it touching for five or ten seconds.

The meteorite felt warm but not hot.

I felt so excited, I started to choke. Coughing and sputtering, I took a deep breath and struggled to calm down.

But how could I calm down? I had just touched a rock from outer space!

"I have to show Mom and Dad!" I said out loud.

Could I pick it up?

It was no longer warm. But how heavy was it?

I wiped my sweaty hands off on the legs of my jeans. Then I bent over the meteorite to lift it.

Whoa. Heavier than I thought.

But I grasped it in both hands and started to raise it off the ground.

And a tiny, shrill voice called out, *"Hey — put me aown!"*

19

"**H**uh?"

I dropped the meteorite onto the grass. It thudded heavily and didn't roll.

I started to bend down to it again. But a high-pitched giggle behind me made me stop.

I spun around. "Billie — ! Was that you? Did *you* say that?"

"Yes. Of course it was me. Who else?" She stepped into the light. Her eyes flashed gleefully.

"What are you doing here?" I demanded.

"I saw you out the window," she replied. "Did I scare you?"

"Maybe," I replied. "You made me drop —"

"What are you doing with that ball?" she demanded, staring down at it.

"It's not a ball," I told her. "It's a meteorite from

outer space. Like they've been talking about on TV."

She laughed. "That's so lame."

"No. Really!" I protested. "It fell from a giant fireball. The light was so bright, I couldn't see a thing."

"Bor-ing," Billie chanted, rolling her eyes.

"Listen to me!" I pleaded. "I heard a whistling sound. It shot down so fast, I thought I was dead meat."

"Bor-ing," Billie repeated. "Jack, it's a stupid ball. Why are you making up this crazy story? The kids are only going to laugh at you."

"It's *true*!" I shrieked. "It fell from the sky!"

"Okay, Saucerman," she replied.

"Stop it!" I shouted.

"Saucerman! Saucerman! Saucerman!" She shouted the name in my face. "Everyone is going to call you that — forever!"

Down on my knees beside the meteorite, I squinted up at her. "You really didn't see it fall from the sky?"

Billie shook her head. "Of course not. How could I see a rubber ball fall from the sky at night?"

I groaned. "It's not rubber. It's a rock, Billie. From outer space."

"Bor-ing," she repeated for the hundredth time. She pretended to yawn.

Mom and Dad will believe me, I told myself.

They never believed me before. But this time I've got proof. This time I've got the real thing!

I lifted the meteorite carefully in both hands.

"You jerk!" Billie cried. "Stop pretending it's heavy."

"It *is* heavy," I groaned. I ignored her laughter and carried the rock up the lawn, walking carefully, gripping it tightly.

Billie followed close behind me, chanting, "Saucerman, Saucerman," the whole way.

I burst into the house and ran into the den. Mom and Dad turned from the TV. "Jack — ?" Mom started.

"I have it!" I screamed. "What they've been talking about on the news! A meteorite! From outer space! It landed right next to me! It fell out of a giant fireball! And I have it! I have it!"

They both stared across the room at the rock in my hands.

"A croquet ball?" Mom asked Dad.

Dad raised his eyes to me. "Is it a shot put?"

I swallowed hard, trying to catch my breath. "No way!" I cried. "It fell from the sky! It's a meteorite! A real meteorite!"

"I saw *two* of them!" Billie declared. "No — five. They fell from the moon!"

"Billie — go to another room," Dad ordered in his sternest voice.

Billie knew not to argue with that voice. She turned and hurried away.

My parents walked over to me, their expressions worried. Dad put a hand on my shoulder. "It's okay, Jack. We understand that you're upset."

"Those news shows on TV are very upsetting," Mom said softly, biting her bottom lip. "They frightened you. But you're going to be okay."

"Yes, you're going to be just fine," Dad echoed, nodding.

"But it's a *meteorite* — !" I insisted, holding the heavy rock up to them.

"Go up to your room and change into your pajamas," Mom said softly, running a hand through my hair. "Get into bed, and I'll be up there in a second."

"Put the ball away somewhere," Dad added. "I can see that it's upsetting you."

"It's not a ball!" I wailed.

"You're going to be fine," Mom said. "We're going to take good care of you."

"You're going to be fine, Jack," Dad agreed. "We'll have Dr. Bendix check you out in the morning. Don't worry — okay?"

I opened my mouth to reply. But what was the point?

They'd never believe me. Never. Not even with a meteorite from outer space stuck right under their noses!

I didn't argue anymore. I slumped up the stairs to my room.

I could hear Billie somewhere downstairs, chanting a made-up song as loudly as she could:

Saucerman, Saucerman, where did you go?
To Jupiter and Mars, to find a rubber ball. . . .

I *hate* it when Billie makes up songs. They're so bad. They don't even rhyme.

I trudged into my room and slammed the door behind me as hard as I could. "You're *all* stupid," I muttered bitterly. "Someday soon, you'll *all* have to apologize for not believing me. And guess what? I won't *accept* your dumb apologies!"

I set the meteorite down carefully in the center of my dresser top. I made sure it wasn't going to roll off. Then I changed into my pajamas.

I started to climb into bed when I heard the voices.

The tinny, high voices.

I gasped.

I don't have the little box anymore, I realized. I returned it to Mr. Fleshman.

But I'm hearing the voices, anyway!

That means they're *inside my head*!

I really *am* crazy!

covered my ears, but I could still hear the voices.

So close. They sounded so much closer now.

Their voices chirped clearly over the whistle of static. And I could understand them.

They are coming, I realized.

They say they are coming soon.

The static hissed. The shrill voices rose and fell.

I pressed the pillow over my head. But I couldn't drown them out.

You will help us, I heard clearly, so clearly that the words sent chills running down my back. *You will help us. You will be ready. You will follow the plan.*

"I will follow the plan," I repeated in a choked whisper.

And then I cried out, "No!"

I had to fight them. I had to keep them from controlling me.

But how?

The voices seemed to circle me, to swirl around me.

You will be ready.

You will help us take root.

Our roots shall spread. You will follow the plan.

"Yes," I whispered. "Yes."

But I gritted my teeth and tried to resist. I tried to stay *me*. Jack Archer.

Jack Archer will not be a slave, I told myself. Jack Archer will not obey them. Will not help them.

As the voices echoed in my ears, I repeated my name over and over. As long as I know who I am, I decided, I will be okay.

I sat on the edge of the bed, every muscle in my body tight. "I have to warn people," I said out loud. "I have to let people know that they are coming to Earth."

But, how? Who will believe me?

My own parents think I'm a nutcase. I heard them downstairs leaving a phone message for Dr. Bendix.

Who will believe me?

You will be ready for us.

You will help us spread our roots.

You will guide us to a quick victory.

Victory . . . victory . . .

"Yes, I will be ready!" I cried.

I shuddered. They sounded so close. When did they plan to come here? When would they land on our planet?

A wild idea flashed into my mind. I remembered a radio call-in show my dad sometimes has on in the car. People call in and talk about UFO sightings and *Star Trek* and *Star Wars* and stuff like that.

I clicked on the clock radio on my bed table. Music poured out. It drowned out the chirp of voices in my head.

I turned down the volume so that Mom and Dad couldn't hear. Then I flipped from station to station until I found the call-in show.

A caller was talking about Klingons from some *Star Trek* episode. I listened for the phone number. Then I dialed it.

The first six times I tried, the line was busy. On the seventh try, I got through.

"Out of This World," a woman with a very soft, pleasant voice said. That's the name of the show. "What would you like to talk about?"

"They're coming!" I cried. "The Others are coming!"

"What is your name?" she asked calmly.

"Jack Archer!" I told her, my voice cracking. "I have to warn everyone. Please — there isn't much time. They're going to land on Earth — soon!"

"How old are you, Jack?" she asked.

"I'm twelve," I said. "But that's not important. I have to warn everyone. You have to listen to me. The voices told me. The voices told me they are coming soon!"

Silence for a moment. And then the woman said in her soft, pleasant voice, "Jack, would you do me a really big favor?"

"Excuse me?" I cried. "A favor?"

"Yes," she said. "A really big favor?"

"What favor?" I asked.

"Would you please call back in about ten years?"

"But — but — but —" I sputtered.

I heard a click. Then the buzz of the dial tone in my ear.

My heart pounding, I slammed the phone down onto the bed table. "She didn't believe me," I muttered angrily.

Who would believe me? Who would help?

I pulled a writing pad and a pencil from the bed table drawer. I decided to make a list of people who might listen, who might help.

I wrote: *1) Parents*.

I had to try them one more time.

2) Mr. Liss. He's my science teacher. I should have thought of him before. He's very smart and knows everything there is to know about all kinds of science.

3) Mr. Fleshman. He probably wouldn't believe me. But he was the only other person I could think of who might listen.

Anyone else?

Anyone?

No. I couldn't think of a single person. But, for some reason, making the list helped to calm me down.

I clicked off the lamp and settled into bed. Across the room, the meteorite on the dresser gave off a soft glow.

I'll bring that in to Mr. Liss, I decided. That will show him that I'm not making everything up. Maybe it will make him believe that something strange is going on.

Gazing at the meteorite, the voices buzzing in my ears, I fell into an exhausted sleep.

It seemed like only minutes later that Mom was calling upstairs for me to wake up. I pulled on jeans and a T-shirt and hurried down to the kitchen. I said good morning to Mom and Dad, who were sitting at the counter, sipping from white mugs of coffee.

I sat down in my place. And took a deep breath.

One more try, I told myself. I'm going to speak softly and calmly now. And I'm going to try one last time to make them believe me.

I looked up to find both of them studying me. "How are you feeling this morning, Jack?" Mom asked.

"Fine," I replied. I took another deep breath. "I feel okay," I said. "But there *is* something I have to tell you."

"Yes. What is it?" Dad replied, leaning over the table.

"Well . . . ," I began.

And Billie came bursting into the room, shouting. "I found a meteorite! I found a meteorite! Look! I found one too!"

21

et *me* see that!" I cried.

Did she really find another meteorite? Did she?

I grabbed it from her hand. And studied it carefully.

And let out a groan.

It was just an old rubber ball we used to play with.

"Let me see it," Dad said. He took it from me and rolled it over in his hands and pretended to study it.

Billie stuck out her tongue at me. "See? I found one too." She sneered.

"But mine is *real*!" I screamed. "Mine is *real*!"

I planned to stay calm. But how could I?

Once again, Billie had ruined everything. Now they would never take me seriously. Never.

"AAAAAAGH!" I let out a frustrated cry and leaped up from the table.

"Jack — finish your breakfast," Mom ordered.

But I ignored her and ran out of the room. I flew up the stairs two at a time. Pulled on my backpack. Grabbed the meteorite off the dresser. And darted out of the house.

I could hear my parents calling after me. But I didn't care. I had to find someone to believe me. I could be the one person who knew the truth.

The whole planet could be in trouble, I told myself. The whole planet could be invaded by alien creatures from outer space.

And my parents would rather pretend that Billie's rubber ball was a meteorite!

Mr. Liss will believe me, I told myself. And he's a science teacher. So people will listen to him.

I jogged across the street, squinting into the bright morning sunlight. Marsha and Maddy came running up beside me.

Maddy glanced at the meteorite in my hand. "Are you still messing around with clay?" she asked. "You're not going to throw *that* one at the window — are you?"

I didn't think that was funny. But they both giggled.

I tried to explain to them. "It's not clay. It fell from the sky. It's some kind of meteorite."

"Jack fell from the sky," Marsha told Maddy.

"Yeah. And he fell on his head!"

They both thought that was hilarious.

"I think aliens sent this meteorite down as a warning," I told them. "Or maybe to test the atmosphere. To see if it is safe to land here."

Marsha and Maddy didn't laugh this time. They both stared hard at me.

"Come on, Jack. We know you don't really believe this stuff," Maddy said.

"It's all true. You'll see!" I snapped. I ran on ahead. I didn't need to hear any more of their laughter and bad jokes.

I carried the meteorite carefully in both hands. As I ran into school, I saw some kids pointing at me and laughing.

I headed upstairs to the science lab. "Mr. Liss?" I called. "Mr. Liss? I have to show you —"

Not there.

I didn't have science class for another two hours. I knew I couldn't carry the meteorite around with me all morning. So I tucked it away on a cluttered shelf in the back of the room.

Then I hurried to Mrs. Hoff's classroom.

The morning dragged on. I didn't hear a word she said. I stared at the clock, waiting for science class. Waiting for my chance to talk to Mr. Liss.

I'll be very calm, I decided. I'll try to sound like a scientist.

First, I'll show him the meteorite. Then I'll tell

him about the voices in my head. Then I'll tell him that the voices warned me.

Then Mr. Liss and I will figure out the best way to alert everyone that the aliens are coming.

"Can you solve it, Jack?" Mrs. Hoff's voice broke into my thoughts. I gazed around the room. Why was everyone grinning at me?

"Well? Can you solve it?" the teacher demanded.

What is she talking about? I wondered.

"No," I replied.

Everyone laughed.

Mrs. Hoff laughed too. "I think I caught you daydreaming," she said.

"I guess," I replied.

So what's the big deal? I've got things on my mind. Important things.

That's what I wanted to say. But, instead, I just sat there and let everyone laugh at me.

As soon as the bell rang, I jumped up from my seat. I wanted to fly up the stairs to the science lab.

But Mrs. Hoff called me back to make sure I wasn't daydreaming when she gave out the homework assignment.

By the time I got to the science lab, it was already full. Kids were in their seats, pulling out their science notebooks. Mr. Liss was talking to some kids at the front of the room.

Finally! I thought. Finally, I can show the meteorite to him and tell him what is happening.

I dropped my backpack. Hurried to the shelf in back of the room where I had stashed the meteorite.

And let out a horrified scream.

The meteorite! It was gone!

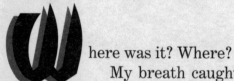

here was it? Where?

My breath caught in my throat. My knees started to buckle.

I heard laughter.

I spun around and saw Henry in the aisle next to the windows. He grinned at me. Then he raised his hand. He had the meteorite in it.

"Hey — give me that!" I cried.

"Come and get it, Saucerman!" Henry called.

I dove across the room to grab it. Henry heaved it to Derek.

I leaped at Derek.

He threw it back to Henry.

Kids were laughing and cheering.

"Be careful with that!" I pleaded. "It's not a ball! Really! It's not a ball!"

Henry threw it to Maddy. She held it out to me. "Here you go, Saucerman!"

I grabbed for it — and she rolled it to Derek. Derek heaved it across the room to Marsha.

"No — please!" I shrieked. "Don't drop it! It's a meteorite from outer space! Don't drop it!"

I don't think anyone could hear me. The entire room was in an uproar. Kids were cheering. Begging Marsha to throw it to them. Clapping and laughing.

And chanting, "Saucerman! Saucerman! Saucerman!"

"Please — stop!" I cried, my voice tight with panic.

"Over here! Over here!" Henry shouted, waving to Marsha.

"No — !" I begged.

Marsha heaved the meteorite across the room to Henry.

I made a wild dive, trying to intercept it.

Missed.

Henry missed too. It slipped through his hands.

And sailed out the open window.

Kids went wild, shouting, cheering, and clapping.

For a moment, I froze. I stared out the window where the meteorite had vanished.

Then I heard the voices. The high-pitched voices ordering me. *"Jump! Jump! Jump!"*

I climbed up on the window ledge.

"DON'T!" I heard Marsha scream.

I stared down — five stories down. A long fall. Too far to jump.

I started to get dizzy. Wobbly. Teetering, now. About to fall out the window.

Can't. Can't jump.

"Jump! Jump! Jump!" the voices commanded.

"Saucerman thinks he can fly!" Derek yelled.

"Stop him!" Maddy shouted. "Someone, stop him!"

"Jump! Jump! Jump!" the voices commanded. *"Jump! Jump! JUMP!"* they screamed inside my head.

"Yes!" I shouted. "YES! I WILL OBEY!"

23

"Nooooo!" I heard someone scream. Then I realized it was me. "NO! I will not jump!" I fought back. "I will not!"

I stepped off the window ledge. I shook my head hard, trying to shake free of the voices. Shake free of their control.

My heart pounding, I spun away from the window. Faced a sea of staring eyes. Heard a wave of hushed whispers.

Pushing kids out of my way, I tore out of the science lab. Down the stairs, my sneakers echoing in the empty stairwell. And out the front door to the school.

Where is it? I asked myself, my eyes frantically searching the ground.

It fell from the fifth floor. Did it break? Did it smash into powder?

"Yes!" I let out a scream when I saw it. Resting in the tall grass.

I dove for it. Grabbed it up to examine it. The meteorite was okay.

I cradled it carefully in my hands. The sound of voices made me look up to the fifth floor. Kids were leaning out of the science lab window, calling down to me.

"Saucerman! Saucerman! Saucerman!" The chant floated out over the school grounds.

Mr. Liss stared out the window too. Stared at me, shaking his head in disgust.

Something inside me snapped. I couldn't take it anymore.

It was the sight of Mr. Liss, the disbelief in his eyes as he gazed down at me.

Now he thinks I'm crazy too. Now he will never believe the truth.

"Nooooooo!" A painful cry burst from my throat.

Holding the meteorite tightly, I started to run. I darted across the street and kept running.

The kids' shouts followed me. I glanced back and saw Mr. Liss motioning wildly with both hands for me to get back in the school.

But I couldn't go back. I had to get away from their shouts, their cruel and stupid chants.

I ran all the way home. Ran in a blur of green lawns and shimmering gray pavement.

I burst through the front door. No one home in

the middle of the day. Gasping for breath, I climbed up to my room.

I set the meteorite in its place on the dresser top. Then I threw myself facedown on my bed. I buried my hot, sweat-drenched face in my pillow. And struggled to get control, to calm down, to catch my breath.

But the voices returned. The voices called to me.

You will obey.

You will be ready.

We are coming soon.

You will help us to victory.

"Yes!" I cried, pulling myself to my feet. "Yes, I am ready now! Yes, I will help you!"

24

I stood stiffly in the middle of my room and stared at the meteorite. I stared at it until it became a fuzzy blur, shimmering on the dresser top.

"I am ready!" I cried. My voice echoed through the empty house. "I will obey!"

The voices chattered excitedly. I could tell they were arriving soon. They were going to land on Earth any minute.

And then what?

What did they plan to do?

They said they would put down roots. They talked about *victory*. Did that mean they were going to start a war?

Did they plan to hurt us? Did they plan to kill us all?

I strained to hear the voices clearly. But they

110

chattered and chirped so rapidly now — like cartoon chipmunk voices — I couldn't understand them.

Where did the voices come from? I wondered again, standing so stiffly, listening, feeling myself drawn to them, feeling their power slide over me.

Are they really inside my head?

"Command me!" I cried. "I am ready to serve!"

Was that really me saying those weird things?

The voices held me in their power. But every once in a while, I felt like myself for a few seconds. I could think clearly for just a moment.

And in one of those moments, I glimpsed a sheet of paper on my bed table. And I read the names on it. My list. My list of people who might listen, who might believe me.

Mr. Fleshman!

Yes. The last name on the list.

The voices swirled around me. Held me there as if hypnotized. So many voices.

And then they paused for a moment. And I spun around. Whirled away from them. Forced my legs to carry me to the door.

I lurched down the stairs. Out the back door. The sky had turned gray and smoggy. The air felt heavy and damp.

I squeezed through the fence and made my way to Mr. Fleshman's back porch. "You are my last chance," I murmured. "You've *got* to believe me."

I stopped under the back window when I heard Mr. Fleshman's voice. Through the window screen, I saw him pacing the kitchen, holding a cell phone to his ear.

I started to call out to him — but stopped when I heard his words.

"Yes, I am ready," he said into the cell phone.

Huh? Ready?

I pressed myself against the side of the house to hear better.

"I know, I know," Mr. Fleshman said. "I lost the communicator for a while. The boy next door took it. No. He didn't know what he had."

So it *wasn't* a beeper!

Mr. Fleshman had lied.

My heart pounding, I listened to his whispery voice, floating out of the open window.

"I got the communicator back in time," Mr. Fleshman continued. "That's right, General. I can hear them now very clearly."

Through the window, I watched him pacing back and forth, the cell phone pressed against his ear. Suddenly, he turned to the window. His strange gray eyes stared straight at me!

I dropped to the ground. And listened.

Had he seen me?

No.

His conversation continued.

"No problem. No problem," Mr. Fleshman said. "They are here, General. They have started to land. The invasion is under way. Listen to me. I can handle them. They don't stand a chance. Not a chance! We will destroy them all. I promise you can count on me, sir. I'll do my job."

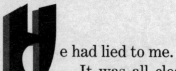

e had lied to me.

It was all clear now. Mr. Fleshman wasn't a special-effects designer. That was his cover. He had all those creatures and ghosts in his house to throw people off the track. He had fooled me for a while.

But now I knew the truth.

Fleshman worked for the government.

Maybe he was in the army. Or maybe he was a special FBI agent assigned to fight aliens.

He said he was ready to fight them. He said it was his job. He promised his boss he would destroy them all.

I took a deep breath and took off back to my house. I made it to the fence and squeezed through the opening.

I have to run up to my room and get the meteorite, I decided. I have to show it to Mr. Fleshman as fast as I can.

He knows about the invasion. He's listened to the voices.

He knows they are coming.

He will know if the aliens sent down this meteorite.

I ran so hard, my side ached. My temples throbbed. Ignoring the pain, I burst into the house and tore up the stairs to my room.

The voices . . .

The voices . . .

I hadn't heard them outside, I realized.

How weird . . .

Sweat poured down my forehead, into my eyes. My side still ached from running.

I started into my room — but stopped in the doorway.

And stared in shock at the meteorite on my dresser.

"It's . . . moving!" I murmured in a choked whisper.

I brushed the sweat from my eyes with the back of my hand. I grabbed the door frame with both hands to steady myself.

A pale green glow radiated from the meteorite. It grew brighter, brighter, like a tiny green sun.

The bright light shimmered in the dresser mirror behind it. Shimmered brighter and brighter until the light filled the mirror.

The green light poured over me.

I shielded my eyes with one hand, gripping the door frame with the other.

The light felt so warm, like a ray of sunlight. It spread through my bedroom until the entire room and everything in it glowed bright green.

And then I saw the meteorite move again.

It trembled and shook.

It spun on the dresser top. Spun in place.

Faster. Faster. Until it became a blur of green light.

Then it slowed to a stop.

I heard a long, loud *CRACK*. Like a walnut being crushed.

A small, square opening appeared on the top of the meteorite.

"Ohhh." A terrified moan escaped my throat. I stumbled into the room, stepped into the shimmering green glow.

And gaped in amazement as a tiny green stick poked up from the opening in the meteorite.

And then another.

No. Not sticks.

Arms. Or maybe legs.

Something was crawling out!

My legs trembled. My chest heaved up and down.

But I took a step closer.

I had to see this. I had to see this creature clearly.

Squinting into the pulsing green light, I watched a slender head pop up in the square opening. Narrow and green and shiny wet.

Like a lizard head.

The two front legs poked out farther. The head tilted back — and sniffed. Breathing the air for the first time.

A narrow green body lifted itself from the opening. An insect body. Almost like a stick figure.

"Ohhhhh." I couldn't hold back a moan of horror. My whole body trembled. I raised both hands to my cheeks and stared across the room at it.

Stared frozen in place as the front legs lowered silently to the dresser top. The rest of the sticklike body slid out quickly. The back legs hit the dresser.

Wet. Sparkling wet. The creature stood on all fours. A little bigger than a grasshopper.

It tilted its head up. Two oval, shiny black eyes gazed up to the ceiling. It sniffed the air again.

Sniffed harder.

The four feet made wet sucking sounds as they took their first steps toward the edge of the dresser.

As I stared in amazement, the feet appeared to grow. To stretch.

The creature took another step. The feet made wet popping sounds with each step.

The slender body thickened. The head appeared to inflate.

The creature was as big as a lizard now.

"I — I don't *believe* this!" I whispered.

A step at a time, it began to lower itself down the front of the dresser. Headfirst.

Growing.

Growing.

Growing as it climbed down.

I saw a thick trail of milky slime on my dresser top. The slime trailed down the front of the dresser behind the creature.

And then I heard the voices again. Chirping excitedly.

Louder now. Much louder.

And I realized the voices came from inside the meteorite.

They weren't inside my head.

I wasn't crazy after all. The voices were real. From inside the meteorite.

The creature landed on the floor on its back feet. The wet feet made a soft *SQUISH* — and spread out over the floor.

The creature stood on its hind legs now. Stretching . . . growing . . . until it stood as tall as the dresser.

Shiny, slender arms slid out below broadening shoulders. Hands formed. Curled into fists at first. Then opening, three fingers on each hand.

The insect head shifted and changed. The oval black eyes grew as large as quarters. A square forehead jutted out. The insect snout pulled back. Now I saw two deep nostrils and a small, lipless mouth.

SQUISH . . . SQUISH . . .

The creature took two steps away from the dresser.

I glimpsed puddles of milky slime on the floor behind it.

It grew taller . . . broader.

It raised its shiny eyes until . . . until . . . *I saw my reflection in its eyes!*

It sees me! I realized.

A real space alien! It sees me!

And as I stared frozen in shock and horror, it pushed out its long arms. Opened its three-fingered hands.

So wet and green . . . glistening like the lawn after a heavy dew.

Still growing . . . still stretching . . . taller than me now!

SQUISHHHHH . . . SQUISSSSHHH . . .

It stuck out its arms.

And came for me.

TO BE CONTINUED

About R.L. Stine

R.L. Stine is the most popular author in America. He is the creator of the *Goosebumps*, *Give Yourself Goosebumps*, *Fear Street*, and *Ghosts of Fear Street* series, among other popular books. He has written nearly 200 scary novels for kids. Bob lives in New York City with his wife, Jane, teenage son, Matt, and dog, Nadine.

Welcome to the new millennium of fear

Check out this
chilling preview of
what's next from
R.L. STINE

Invasion of the
Body Squeezers

Part II

4

"Oh, my," I heard Mr. Liss murmur. "Oh, my. Oh, my."

"See?" I whispered.

Mr. Liss nodded, his mouth open, his eyes bulging. "Oh, my." He swept both hands back through his brown hair.

I swallowed hard. "It's blocking the door," I managed to say in a tiny voice.

"I'm sorry," Mr. Liss whispered. "Sorry I didn't believe you."

The creature hissed and clicked its teeth. Its big eyes rolled around in its head. Its whole body heaved wetly as it took a step away from the door.

"We've got to get away," I said, tugging at the teacher's sleeve. "We've got to get help."

Mr. Liss didn't take his eyes from the alien. "We've got to get a camera!" he declared.

The creature took another heavy step toward us. It stretched its arms out wide, rolling its tube-like fingers. It opened and shut its jaws, its long tusks scraping noisily.

"Mr. Liss, come on!" I insisted. I pulled his arm, trying to tug him toward the back of the house.

But he pulled free of me. "We're going to be famous, Jack," he said breathlessly. "We are the first people on Earth ever to see a being from another planet."

"But if it eats us . . ." I started.

The creature lumbered forward. Its whole body pulsed and bounced as it moved toward us.

"Mr. Liss, please!" I begged.

But the teacher ignored me. He took a step toward the creature. "We are Earthlings!" he shouted to it. "Can you speak? Where are you from?"

The alien stretched out its arms. It opened its mouth in a wet hiss.

"I already tried talking to it!" I declared. "It didn't answer."

I took a step back as the creature moved into the hallway. Closer. Closer.

"Please! We've got to get out!" I shrieked.

Mr. Liss finally turned to me. "I think it's friendly," he said, his voice cracking with excitement.

"Huh?" I gasped.

"I do." The teacher nodded. "I think it's friendly. Look, Jack. It has its arms outstretched. I think it wants a hug."

I took another step back. My heart pounded so hard, I could barely breathe.

"No," I insisted. "It's a trick, Mr. Liss."

"I really think it wants a hug," the teacher replied.

"No! Stay away!" I cried. "It's so ugly! It's so evil!"

Mr. Liss shook his head. "It can't help looking different from us. It's an alien from another planet. But that doesn't mean it's evil."

He took another step toward the pulsing, hissing creature. "I think the alien is trying to greet us, Jack. I think it wants to hug us."

"Mr. Liss — no!" I begged. "Let's go! Please!"

But the teacher ignored my cries.

He stepped forward to greet the alien.

The alien stretched out both its arms. Mr. Liss stretched out both his arms.

And they hugged.

"Oh, my," Mr. Liss murmured.

The creature's green arms wrapped gently around the teacher's shoulders.

"Oh, my," the teacher repeated. "Do you see, Jack? I was right."

Mr. Liss didn't turn around. The creature hugged him tighter. Then it lowered its big green head and pressed it against Mr. Liss's cheek.

"It's a warm-blooded creature, like us," the science teacher reported. "Do you see, Jack? It's friendly. I knew it. I —"

Mr. Liss stopped talking with a gasp.

I saw the creature tighten its arms around him.

"Hey," the teacher groaned. "Wait. Stop —"

The creature's huge head pressed against Mr. Liss's face.

The muscular arms spread around the teacher's slender body.

Tighter.

Mr. Liss groaned again. Then, as I stood behind him watching helplessly, Mr. Liss started to struggle. "Hey, let go! Let go!"

r. Liss!" I cried.

I watched in horror as the creature's powerful arms tightened around the teacher's waist.

Mr. Liss groaned in pain. He struggled and squirmed, trying to wrestle free. His glasses flew off and clattered across the floor. His eyes bulged. His face twisted in terror.

The creature pressed its head against Mr. Liss's cheek and let out short, hissing breaths. *HISS* ... *HISS* ... *HISS* ...

"Can't ... breathe ...," Mr. Liss gasped.

I searched frantically around the hallway for a weapon. Something to throw at the creature. Something to hit it with.

I spotted a tall, glass flower vase on a table outside the living room. I dove for it. Grabbed it in both hands.

I raised it high, preparing to send it crashing down on the creature.

"Noooo!" I let out a scream when I saw the creature's big hands go up. Its tubelike fingers spread. And long silvery nails shot out from the fingers.

The gleaming nails slid out until they were at least a foot long! And then the creature pushed them into Mr. Liss's back.

Mr. Liss uttered a cry. His eyes bulged in horror.

The vase fell from my hands and dropped to the floor with a heavy *THUD*.

I started to choke.

I'm not seeing this! I told myself.

This isn't happening!

The long nails slid straight through the teacher's shirt. Into his back. Slid inside Mr. Liss, as if he were made of air.

I watched its big hands totally slide inside Mr. Liss's back. Then its arms.

The alien lowered a shoulder, hunched its head. The shoulder pushed into the teacher's back. The green head made a wet, slapping sound as it slid inside.

"No! No! No! Oh, no!" Mr. Liss chanted, mouth open wide in fright. His arms shot up in the air. His eyes rolled frantically in his head.

"No! No! No!"

The creature's knees bent. It tilted forward. And then *leaped* off the floor.

Leaped into Mr. Liss's back.

And vanished.

Vanished inside the teacher.

"No! No! No!" Mr. Liss continued to chant. His arms flew wildly above his head.

I staggered back against the wall. My chest heaved. I struggled to breathe. I covered my ears to block out the teacher's horrified chant.

"No! No! No!"

And I stared at Mr. Liss's back.

At his shirt. Smooth now. Not a wrinkle. Not a hole or a tear.

No bulge. No wound. No blood.

The shirt had come untucked in the struggle. It was stained with sweat under the arms. But I could see no sign of the creature.

It had vanished. Pushed itself inside Mr. Liss.

The teacher's cries stopped suddenly. Breathing hard, he lowered his arms. He scrambled to tuck in his shirt.

"Mr. Liss?" I finally managed to call out his name.

He squinted at me, as if not recognizing me. Then he bent and picked up his glasses.

"Mr. Liss? Are you okay?" I choked out, my back still pressed hard against the wall. My legs so trembly and weak.

He slid the glasses onto his face. Then he

brushed back his hair with one hand. He shook his head as if trying to clear it.

Then he started to hum. Softly. Just musical notes. Not a tune. He hummed to himself, staring blankly at me.

"Mr. Liss?" I whispered. "It's me. Jack. Are you okay?"

He continued to hum. Then he smacked his lips together. Smacked them several times, making kissing sounds.

He scratched his right shoulder. Then he scratched the back of his neck. Scratching hard, so hard that the skin reddened.

I've got to get out of here, I decided.

Mr. Liss isn't right. The creature pushed inside him. And now Mr. Liss isn't right.

He started humming again. Just notes, crazy notes. Not a song. As he hummed, he scratched his neck, then his shoulder.

"Uh . . . I'll go get help," I said. I started to slide along the wall toward the front door.

Mr. Liss stopped humming. He lowered his hand and moved to block my path.

He clicked his tongue. "T-t-t. I'm okay, Jack," he said. He spoke so slowly, one word at a time.

"No. I'll get someone," I insisted. "You wait here, Mr. Liss. I'll be back as soon as I find someone to help."

"No. Really," the teacher insisted. A strange,

half-smile formed on his lips. "I'm perfectly t-t okay."

And as he smiled at me, something green bulged out of both of his ears. It looked like bubble gum bubbles, inflating. Like green balloons growing out of his ears.

"I — I'll get a doctor or someone," I stammered, inching toward the open door.

"T-t-t. I don't need a doctor," he replied, still smiling. "I've never felt better, Jack." The green bubbles bobbed on both sides of his face. Then they silently deflated and slid back into his ears.

"It's *inside* you!" I screamed. The words burst from my mouth. I had controlled my panic for so long. But I couldn't hold it in any longer.

"The alien disappeared! It went *inside* you, Mr. Liss. I saw it!"

He shook his head. "No. I'm t-t-t fine." He took a step toward me, that strange half-smile frozen on his face. Behind his glasses, his eyes stared straight ahead at me. They didn't move. They didn't blink.

The green bubbles poked out of his ears again. Bobbed for a few seconds. Then disappeared back into his head.

"I'm going for help!" I cried.

But he blocked my way.

"Don't t-t be afraid, Jack," he said softly.

"I *am* afraid!" I shrieked. "It's inside you, Mr. Liss. Don't you understand? I've got to get help!"

He shook his head again. Then he spread out his arms. His eyes burned into mine. "Give me a hug, Jack," he whispered.

"Huh?" I gasped and stepped back.

"Give me a t-t hug," the teacher repeated, stretching out his arms. "It wants to spread itself to you too. Then it will be inside both of us."

"No —" I gasped.

"It wants to t-t-t spread out, to spread itself to everyone," Mr. Liss continued. "Won't that be *wonderful*?"

He stepped toward me, his shoes scraping heavily over the floor. Green bubbles poked from his ears, then slid back in.

I took another step back. Then another.

"Just a quick hug," Mr. Liss insisted. He clicked several times. "A quick hug, Jack. We have to spread out. We have to hug everyone. It's okay. Really. T-t. I'm perfectly okay."

My back hit the wall. "No — please!" I cried. "I don't want to. You're *not* okay! You're *weird*! You're *possessed*!"

"No," he replied softly, shuffling closer. His shoes scraped along the floor, as if they were too heavy for him to lift.

"A quick hug, Jack," he insisted. "Be one of the first. You're so lucky to be one of the first."

"Noooo!" I wailed.

I pushed myself off the wall and sprang past him, into the living room. And cried out when I saw Mom and Billie enter from the back. "You're home!"

Mom dropped her briefcase on the table and turned to me. "Jack? What's going on? Why are you home so early?"

I spun around and pointed at Mr. Liss with a trembling hand. "He's got the *creature* inside him!" I shrieked. "Stop him! Stop him! It's *inside* him!"

GET READY.

The aliens have landed.
Their mission: To squeeze you dry.

GOOSEBUMPS®
SERIES 2000
R.L. STINE

The Continuing Story...

Book #5: Invasion of the Body Squeezers: Part II

The next millenium will shock you.

In bookstores this May.

◣ SCHOLASTIC   ✳ PARACH

THE SPINE-TINGLING VIDEO SERI BASED ON YOUR FAVORITE BOOK

Goosebumps ™

R.L. STINE

Goosebumps
NIGHT OF THE
LIVING DUMMY III

BASED ON BOOK #40

Enter the Goosebumps™
SAIL WITH THE STARS® **SWEEPSTAKES**
for a chance to win a
cruise for four to
Walt Disney World
with R.L. Stine!
No purchase necessary.
Sweepstakes begin January 13, 1998
and end May 1, 1998. For details, call
1-800-942-2287

NO
ON VI
AT O
$14
OR LESS E

WATCH THE NEW ULTIMATE GOOSEBUMPS™ SATURDAY MORNING ON FOX KIDS NETWORK!